Baby
Elephant
Diet

Ravi Mantha is a health guru who is an expert on prevention and wellness. He speaks at conferences around the world on how to take control of our own health and bodies. Ravi is a strong proponent of sustainable agriculture, an organic farmer and a foodie. This is his second book on health. He can be reached on twitter@rmantha2

The Baby Elephant Diet

A Modern Indian Guide to
EATING RIGHT

RAVI MANTHA

RUPA

Published by
Rupa Publications India Pvt. Ltd 2015
7/16, Ansari Road, Daryaganj
New Delhi 110002

Sales Centres:
Allahabad Bengaluru Chennai
Hyderabad Jaipur Kathmandu
Kolkata Mumbai

ISBN: 978-81-291-3745-6

First impression 2015

10 9 8 7 6 5 4 3 2 1

The moral right of the author has been asserted.

Printed by Parksons Graphics Pvt. Ltd. Mumbai

Contents

Foreword

After the success of my first book *All about Bacteria*, I received numerous queries from my readers, with most of them asking, 'What about nutrition?' If my first book on health dealt with what lives on your body, this book is about what you put into your body every day, and its health implications. As before, my modus operandi was to study historical perspectives on nutrition, combine these with the latest research in nutrition science, and give you practical and useful tips on daily living so you can live a long and healthy life.

I am a gourmand, a man who likes to enjoy life to the fullest. There is nothing I like more than a delicious meal made with fresh ingredients and enjoyed in the company of family and friends. You will see that I am always biased in favour of taste as well as nutrition. Food is not just about sustenance, it is about joie de vivre or the very joy of living, and it must always be consumed in that context. But if you are someone who just eats for sustenance, that's all right too... in fact, this attitude will make it easier for you to choose the right foods to eat, and this book will help you make healthy choices.

I write not as a nutrition scientist but as an inquisitive individual. Plenty of scientific research today is funded and controlled by special interest groups that usually have a commercial goal. As you will see in this book, I have the opposite aim. Every solution you will see in this book is designed to keep you healthy, and these home solutions will be easy on your pocket too. Yes, I do endorse products that I genuinely believe are good for you, but I have never accepted any incentive for doing so (and if I ever receive any in future, I will disclose it).

I am not a new-age writer. As with all my work, unless stated otherwise, I have attempted to place this book firmly within the realm of the scientific method, citing published works where appropriate. I have tried to differentiate fact from conjecture and anecdotes from statistical evidence. But science itself is a process of discovery, hypothesis, conjecture, testing and finally proof. In the field of nutrition, most experts have a one-size-fits-all approach; hence they come up with universal pronouncements like 'eat a big breakfast' or 'eat six small meals a day'. But we are not all made the same way.

Nutrition science is evolving all the time, so there may be areas where I will be proven wrong or lacking as science advances. But I can assure you that if you follow the simple guidelines on nutrition in this book, you will dramatically improve your health. This work is a follow-on to my bestselling book *All about Bacteria* which explored the various ways the trillions of microbes on our body help us maintain our health. I hope you get a chance to read that book as well.

Fond wishes and good health!

Ravi Mantha

Introduction

How the Baby Elephant Became Ganesha, Our Friend, Our Dietitian and the God of New Beginnings

Have you ever wondered what it is about a baby elephant that makes you smile? Why is the most popular deity in Hinduism the mischievous one with the elephant head? Why do Hindus associate wisdom, intelligence, pre-eminence and fondness with someone they call the leader of all the classes of beings or Ganapati? This is not a story about Vignesha the controller of obstacles, but it is a popular science tale about how his living representative on our planet, the baby elephant, can inspire you to transform your body by eating right.

You can call it the Ganesha Diet after Lord Ganesha if you like, but it is really just the Baby Elephant Diet, and it will be a game-changer for you.

I know many of you will smile knowingly at my unapologetic attempt to use what biologists call 'charismatic mega fauna' to sell you a health and diet concept. But there is a lot more substance to it than that. The baby elephant may be an adorable animal that also happens to be the living incarnation of Hinduism's most popular god (even more popular than cricketer Sachin Tendulkar!), but soon you will understand why the Baby Elephant Diet is so brilliant for health.

First of all, the baby elephant eats a lot. It never counts calories or thinks about restricting itself. You must have seen enough diets that tell you how many calories there are in each item, and frankly those kinds of diets are really tiresome. The Baby Elephant Diet doesn't work like that at all. In fact, as you will see later on, you will actually be able to increase the quantity of food you eat once you start following this diet. Now who doesn't want to follow a diet where you pretty much do not have to think about every calorie you are eating? In the Baby Elephant Diet, calorie counting is out, and eating the right foods is in.

Second, the baby elephant eats lots and lots of fibre. Have you ever seen a pile of elephant dung? It has so much fibre that there is actually a company, Elephantdungpaper.com, that makes paper out of elephant dung. Each elephant produces enough dung to make over 100 sheets of paper a day! Looking at it another way, only 4 per cent of what an elephant eats has nutritional content that is absorbed by its body. The other 96 per cent gets digested, and then passes right through as fertilizer. The fundamental secret of healthy living that the baby elephant is teaching us is 'eat more fibre'.

Third, the baby elephant is a vegetarian, although it becomes vegan when it stops drinking its mother's milk. In this regard, we are not strictly baby elephants. Humans must have some animal protein even as adults, whether it is dairy or eggs or fish, although we don't need much of it. Indian vegetarians who consume dairy do just fine. While referring to the fast bowling attacks of former Indian cricketers Javagal Srinath and Venkatesh Prasad who are pure vegetarians, a famous commentator would complain that so much vegetarianism in

India meant that we could not produce really fast bowlers—implying that one must eat meat to build muscle. This is complete nonsense. While it is true that one must eat protein to build muscle, there is plenty of research that shows that you can eat vegetable or dairy protein (as many Indian vegetarians do) and be as strong as anybody. You don't have to eat meat. In fact, Patrik Baboumian, one of the strongest men in the world, is a vegan, just like the baby elephant. If you doubt that vegetarians can be strong, just ask an elephant or a rhino or a hippo...but do it from a very safe distance. The strongest beasts in the animal kingdom are all vegans, and they can get quite grumpy if they don't get their daily plant fix.

Now this book is not about vegetarianism. I am not opposed to people eating some animal products (if they choose to), as long as we as a society make good rules about the humane treatment of farm animals and we make an effort to get away from the destructive and inhumane practices of factory farming. But I definitely think that we can quite substantially lower our meat consumption without feeling that we are giving up a source of pleasure, and at the same time have a positive impact on the environment.

Fourth, the baby elephant does not eat processed junk. This is the best teaching of all. Learn what is the meaning of processed food first (you will be surprised to know, for example, that white rice and all flour is highly processed), and then take action to follow the elephant's lead, and minimize the amount of processed food that you put into your mouth. The more processed a food is, the less fibre it has.

And fifth and last of all, the baby elephant leads a full life—it has a lifespan similar to humans—and it does so in very good health. You don't see obese elephants in the wild, and you don't see sick elephants in the wild. They just go on and on with their lives, in excellent shape, until they grow old and go to sleep one day and never wake up. What a wonderful way to live, and what a great role model to emulate!

So, taking the lead from our friend and mentor Lord Ganesha and his envoy on earth, let us begin our journey to understanding what food is, and how to interact with it in ways that will bring joy, great health and a positive attitude towards life.

Why We Eat What We Eat: Food Habits

How We Learned to Eat the Right Plants

Have you ever wondered how humans figured out what is edible and what is not? When it comes to eating animals, the answer is quite simple. Our ancestors typically went with taste, because pretty much anything that moves is edible for human consumption. Of course, there are a few exceptions such as the liver of fugu, or Japanese puffer fish, which contains a deadly nerve poison. But generally speaking, you can eat the flesh of any animal, fish or bird, and it won't kill you. The only risks to eating meat are parasites which may be present but are not lethal to humans. If the meat is properly handled and cooked, it is extremely safe and can provide a very nutritious meal.

What about plants? Most plants are actually poisonous to humans or, at the very least, inedible. If you consider the fact that about 90 per cent of what we eat comes directly or indirectly from five plant species, you will begin to appreciate the thousands of years of trial and error that went into working out which plants were safe to eat. In fact, the entire history of agriculture is a patchwork of largely successful attempts to engineer non-poisonous and edible versions of otherwise poisonous plant species for us to grow and eat.

When Michelangelo, one of the greatest sculptors the world has ever seen, was asked how he had created his masterpiece, *David*, his response was: 'It was actually very simple. I saw this block of marble that was hiding David inside, and all I had to do was remove from it all the bits that were not David.'

While ordinary mortals would look at a block of marble and see, well, just a big stone, Michelangelo looked at it and saw a statue of David that was covered with extra marble that he chipped away, revealing a masterpiece. Fundamentally, the world of nutrition is akin to a mound of amazing, tasty, edible foods, and all you have to do is remove the bits that are damaging to your health. If you do this, you will end up with a varied diet that is healthy, nourishing and above all enhances your joy in living and sharing a meal.

Unfortunately today, the reverse is happening. We throw away the healthy portions of plants—seeds and fruit—and eat the sugar junk. Orange pulp is healthy whereas orange juice is just sugar water, but guess what people consume? Similarly, the rice grain has three parts: husk which is fibre, whey which is protein and kernel which is sugar. We tend to throw away the first two parts! This book will open your eyes to what goes into your mouth.

Leaves and Shoots Are Not What the Plant Wants You to Eat

Here is an amazing truth. You may think of plants as existing for your personal eating pleasure, but actually plants have evolutionary goals of their own, and they see us as creatures that they can harness for their own benefit. Plants want to do what every other creature wants to do, which is to grow and multiply and live to the fullest extent of their lifespan. Unlike animals, plants are immobile and can't run away from their predators. You would think this was a major handicap, one that might make survival against predators with sharp teeth somewhat difficult. But plants have not only survived, they have thrived. The reason is that to compensate for this handicap, plants have come up with other strategies for survival.

In fact, plants have developed a variety of defences, mechanical, chemical and biological, to keep predators at bay. For example, take a look at roses and see the way their thorns are an effective deterrent against animals that munch on bushes. The reason most trees have no leaves at ground level is to deter grazing animals, while grass grows thickly together so that predators can't get to all members of the species, and the survivors can then reproduce. This is the same reason why trees produce so many seeds. The idea is that if they can overwhelm the predators with seeds, then at least some of the seeds will survive and find some favourable place to germinate. But the relationship between plants and animals goes way beyond this.

We all know that flowers produce nectar so that bees and other insects are drawn to them and pollination is the happy result for the plant. But imagine that you are a seed and you want a safe place to germinate and grow into a plant. Your best option is to be covered with something that animals want to eat, so that you can make your way into the animal, along with the animal's dinner. The animal or bird will eventually deposit you inside a highly fertile and moist pile of manure far from the parent plant. Perfect!

The reason we are interested in this mutually beneficial

existence is that we are similar to animals, evolutionarily speaking. Plants that have humans as their symbiotic friends want them to eat fruits and seeds, and so they go out of their way to make these fruits and seeds palatable. We are also totally adapted to this relationship. We are supposed to eat a high amount of fibre filled with assorted nutrients, with carbohydrates, fats and proteins thrown into the mix.

But leaves are a different matter. In actual fact, plants don't have any interest in humans or other creatures eating their leaves, and go to extraordinary lengths to make these leaves and shoots toxic for consumption. We humans, on the other hand, have an innate awareness of this tendency, and avoid eating leaves or even berries of unknown plants.

What Is a Diet?

We are all on a diet, all the time. Many of my friends are on what we jokingly call the 'See Food' diet; they see food and they eat it.

Diets are largely cultural. Americans are on the standard American diet (with the apt acronym SAD). Japanese eat a diet rich in seafood protein, fermented foods and fibrous vegetables, and live longer than anyone else. Indians are on what I call the rice (or chapathi) and curry diet. Most of us have a fixed notion of what we definitely do not eat. Indians are mostly either vegetarians who eat dairy, or non-vegetarians who eat chicken, goat and fish.

But the word diet has negative connotations and makes you feel you should restrict yourself, limit your choices, or be austere. If you are not 'dieting', you feel guilty. My goal is to completely alter this mindset. Your body is your temple, and the food you eat is the offering you are making to it. I want you to enjoy the most varied and nutritious and tasty meals that you can find. The only issue is that you must restrict consumption of a few foods to once a week or so. The key to a good diet is to stay positive. In other words, think not so much about what you should not eat, but what you can eat.

I walked into a restaurant recently, a bit late, and found my colleague had already ordered a vegetarian club sandwich with French fries. Now this colleague is young, a bit full-figured, and believes that because she is a vegetarian, she eats healthy. The food that arrived was anything but healthy, and she expected me to share her meal.

I did. I expertly unpacked my half of the club sandwich, discarded the bread, and ate the vegetables. French fries are basically not food, and I lost my craving for them a long time ago (you will too, after about six months of changing your approach to food). While my colleague ate her half of the club sandwich and all the fries, I only ate what I considered to be edible, which was the vegetables in a delicious mayonnaise sauce. I then ordered a burger on a half bun, and ate it with ketchup and mayonnaise.

I realize that it takes a lot of time and effort for most people to get to a point where they can see a plate of freshly prepared French fries and not eat them (or maybe eat one or two). That's okay. I achieved this goal by eating more and more of the right foods and less and less of the wrong foods over time, until my body adjusted and my cravings naturally diminished. That really is all there is to it, but it takes time and patience.

Why Most Diets Fail

Have you ever seen a baby elephant that deliberately goes hungry or goes on a diet? There is a simple reason why most diets fail.

Hunger

People get hungry when they are dieting, and that hunger eventually becomes a raging fire inside their minds which they have to put out with sweets or savoury snacks. Hunger is a primal emotion. People who are hungry are angry, and their stress hormones are higher. The Baby Elephant Diet does not involve hunger, or at least hunger beyond the first three weeks of detoxifying your body from the poisons that you have been ingesting all this time.

In fact, I tell you to actually *increase* the amount of food you eat, in order to get lighter and fitter. Is it possible that the quantity of food you eat is much less important than the quality of it, in terms of its impact on the body? Yes, it most certainly is. If you feel that what I am saying is counter-intuitive, then I want you to do a small experiment. Go to the nearest balcony or terrace this evening with a glass of red wine (or a salted lime soda if you don't drink alcohol), sit in a comfortable place, look up at the setting sun and contemplate your life thus far. Look at the sun, and you will see a most counter-intuitive thing. The sun will clearly move across the horizon and disappear beneath it. In reality, the sun does not revolve around the earth, and it is the earth rotating on its own axis that gives you that illusion. Fully 26 per cent of Americans, in a recent study, said they believed the sun goes around the earth. I am sure many other people around the world would give the same response if the survey were held in other countries.

This book will break many of your so-called dietary beliefs and ideas along the way and cut through all the bad advice that you have been fed so far, both figuratively and literally. I will prove through the weight of science that eating right is not blindly following your parents' diet, or following the marketing jargon of the sugar and processed food industry, or getting seduced by junk processed food masquerading as 'taste bhi aur health bhi'.

One of the most successful social programmes in India is the school midday meal programme run by the Akshaya Patra Foundation, which feeds about thirty lakh children daily. The meal is a simple vegetarian one—dal, one vegetable and some rice or a chapati—tailored to the cuisine of the region where the school is located. The children can have as many servings as they like. Akshaya Patra, which I am familiar with because my wife Kavitha was its first executive director in the UK and helped to develop the donor network there, has sound knowledge about nutrition and children. It knows that children are more attentive in school, and their learning, retention, memory and test scores improve if they are provided a free lunch. Hungry kids are angry kids, and angry kids are not interested in learning.

The point is that it does not take much to improve our nutrition and make the shift to good health. Most of us actually have a problem of plenty—we have too much food to eat, but of the wrong kind, so we become unhealthy and unfit. My aim is to bring you back to basics. Start with eating simple basic food, eliminate junk food from your diet, and you will go from a Jupiter-like girth to Venus-like svelteness in no time at all. Next, I want to reorient your taste buds so that you develop an appreciation for healthy food, enjoy what you eat and eat only what you enjoy. I want your relationship with food to change. Instead of food being superficially comforting but hugely damaging to you, I want it to be healthy and nourishing.

'If you are looking for an austere, severe, punishment-style diet, you are reading the wrong book. Have you ever met a baby elephant that starves itself? I certainly haven't. On the Baby Elephant Diet, you can eat pretty much whenever you like (except late at night). You can eat as much food as you like, as long as it is the right kind of food. This is why it succeeds where most diets fail. You get to eat when you want, as much as you want. You get to be in control of your body and mind, and retain the choice to eat bad foods once in a while. You won't end up with cravings, and you won't end up messing up your food habits.

Why a Crash Diet Is One of the Worst Things You Can Do to Your Body

Most people think that if they simply reduce their food consumption, they will lose body fat. This is partly true. The problem is that if you go on a crash diet and stop eating protein, you will lose not only body fat, you will also lose body muscle. This is a bad idea, because once you stop your diet, the muscle does not come back, but instead is replaced by twice the amount of body weight in fat.

Here's a simple example. A fifty-year old woman weighing 72 kg needs around 1400 calories a day to maintain her weight. Let's say she goes on a crash diet that involves eating only 800 calories a day. What will happen is that she will lose 2 kg in a month. But a significant portion of it—up to two-thirds—will be muscle loss. Having lost 1.3 kg of muscle, she now feels weaker, so starts eating high-carbohydrate foods the moment she gets off the diet. At the end of the second month, she has regained 3.5 kg of fat, and her new 'normal' weight is now 73.3 kg. This happened because the muscle she lost has gone for good and has been replaced by twice the weight in fat.

Isn't this a dreadful way to treat your body? Now, at the end of two months, she weighs 1.3 kg more than she did when she started, has 1.3 kg less muscle and her bone density has also decreased. This is in addition to the toxins she dumped into her liver and kidneys when her body broke down the muscle. She would have been far better off not going on the crash diet at all.

Have you ever wondered why there is such conflicting information about what we should eat? How diet plans such as Atkins, Dukan, South Beach and others promote low-carb diets with equal success? Why Weight Watchers promotes a low-fat, quantity controlled diet and has built a huge business empire doing so? Can all these diet plans be right? The simple truth is that all these methods can work...depending on exactly what you mean by weight loss.

Here is an interesting fact that we don't often think about when we talk of weight loss. Someone with 30 per cent body fat can be the same height and weight as someone with 20 per cent body fat, but the 20 per cent body fat person is much healthier, and much less prone to diabetes and heart disease.

The ideal body fat for good health is less than 18 per cent for men, and less than 25 per cent for women.

This is why I say, 'Do not focus on dropping weight, focus instead on dropping body fat!' These are two completely different goals.

If you followed Weight Watchers or any kind of low-fat or low-calorie diet, and lost five pounds of weight overall, it is likely that all the weight loss came from losing muscle tone because you ate too little protein and too few calories. Your percentage of body fat would have actually gone up! In this case, your diet actually made you more unhealthy even though you lost weight.

Among all the methods of weight loss, I prefer low carb because eating vegetables instead of rice, and fish instead of pasta, is the surest way of losing body fat and bringing down your fat percentage enough to prevent type 2 diabetes.

Why Counting Calories Does Not Work

Sharmi hates exercise, so she is watchful of what she eats and counts calories. She is a busy mom of young children, and has been skipping breakfast for the past two years. Instead, she has two cookies with her morning cup of tea. Is her approach effective for weight loss? The answer is no.

Some of us are very analytical in our approach to life. We use fitness devices to measure the number of steps we take; we count the number of hours of sleep we get; we diligently keep track of our expenses to make sure we are saving each month. It is only natural that we want to count the number of calories we put into our bodies, to get a better sense of what we are eating.

Unfortunately, counting calories does not work. There are enough studies that show that calorie counters do not lose weight. The reason for this is simple: not all calories are the same. In fact, the reason why low-fat diets became so popular a few decades ago is this type of mathematical, and now discredited, approach. Fats have twice the calories by weight compared to other nutrients like protein and carbohydrates, so doctors believed you could lose weight just by reducing your fat intake. This was a simplistic approach. We now know that dietary fat and fat calories have only a minor role to play in weight gain.

A low-carb diet is much better and more effective than a low-fat diet, as science has now recognized.

The point is that your body absorbs and reacts to different foods differently. Calories by themselves don't matter much, since your body weight is determined by genetic factors, sleep, stress levels, inflammation, hormones, and types of gut bacteria. Even more remarkable is the fact that many high-fat foods are actually really good for you. Foods such as whole milk, cheese, avocado, nuts are actually good for weight loss.

The real issue is the hormone insulin, which basically helps your liver convert fast-burning carbs and sugars into body fat. When you eat sugary carbs, the calories in them not only spike your insulin (leading to fat gain), these carbs also get digested really quickly in your small intestine. This is why you can eat a bunch of cookies and still get hungry half an hour later, even though cookies have a lot more calories than, say, fruit.

This is where eating slow-burning carbs and good, healthy fats plays a major role. I have repeatedly stressed that the Baby Elephant Diet is all about changing the composition of the food you eat. It is not about restricting the number of calories you eat, or the quantity of food you eat. Counting calories has no place in modern diet management. Removing refined carbs from your diet should be your primary focus.

Why Six Small Meals a Day Is a Totally Bogus Concept

'Ravi, Ravi, I feel so much better these days,' Aunty Sunita said as she rushed into the room, out of breath.

'My nutritionist suggested that instead of three meals a day, I should have six small meals. This has totally controlled my hypoglycaemia!'

I looked at Aunty Sunita, who was as rotund as ever. This was going to be a long afternoon, I thought to myself.

'But Aunty, did you ask the nutritionist why you should switch to six small meals?'

'Beta, apparently it keeps your blood sugar more stable throughout the day instead of the up and down spikes!'

'Aunty, if that is the case, why are you not getting up four times in the middle of the night to eat small meals?'

Aunty Sunita fell silent.

Let's look at the six meals a day concept and assess whether it makes any sense. Everyone who has ever had a baby knows a simple fact. Babies wake up every two hours and have to feed. For the first few months, they feed up to twelve times a day, which every bleary-eyed mother can attest to. Gradually mothers stop feeding their babies during the night and the babies stop asking for a feed. The result is a lifelong habit of night-time fasting, and thank goodness for that. Imagine waking up every two hours to eat a small meal.

The point is that the human body can adapt to a wide range of diets and mealtimes. People with certain body types don't get hungry in the mornings, and they can live on two meals a day. Some people even live on one meal a day with no noticeable effect on their health. So, what is wrong with having six or even twelve small meals a day, you may ask. The problem is not the body's ability to process food (it can do that just fine whether you eat once or twelve times in a day). The problem is more complex; it is the fact that our bodies have not evolved to consume six meals a day.

There is increasing evidence that intermittent fasting is good for the body, and, on the other side, there is also evidence that people who eat six small meals a day are much fatter than the average person.

The simple fact is that if you are getting your food calories predominantly from good fat and protein, your energy levels tend to be constant throughout the day, and you don't get that gnawing hunger from sugar cravings. But if you are getting your calories from fast-burning carbs and sugar, you will have fluctuating energy levels and you will crave six or even eight meals a day. Ironically, those six meals a day become a vehicle for feeding your sugar addiction. The solution is simple. Get off the sugar addiction!

Animals don't have the luxury of eating six meals a day. In fact, the entire animal kingdom has evolved to survive and thrive on intermittent fasting, because finding food is a hit and miss in the wild. Humans are no different. A recent study shows that overweight people can improve their lipid profiles by reducing the frequency of their meals.[1] It seems clear that only chronically underweight people can benefit from increasing the frequency of their meals, and no one else should be eating six times a day.

I always advocate an outcome-based approach to eating and fitness. If you are dropping body fat or you are already in the optimal health range (below 18 per cent fat for men and 25 per cent for women), then continue doing whatever it is you are doing. If you are getting fat, and staying fat because you are eating six meals a day on the advice of your nutritionist, you need a new nutritionist.

Why We Get Fat as We Get Older...Blame Your Muscles

Your body weight is made up mainly of bone, muscle and fat (and the water within), but let us focus on the muscle and fat, which change with diet and exercise. As discussed earlier, someone with 30 per cent body fat can be the same height and weight as someone with 20 per cent body fat, but the 20 per cent body fat person is much healthier and much less prone to chronic diseases like diabetes and heart disease. What matters is your muscle-to-fat ratio, and not so much your weight or the popular measure known as body mass index (BMI).

BMI has become popular because it is easy to measure.

Just take your weight in kilograms, and divide by the square of your height in metres. This gives a rough indicator of how much body fat you have—your level of obesity. But BMI is very unreliable. People who are muscular and healthy will have a high BMI, similar to the BMI of obese people. This is why I have discarded its use. I prefer percentage body fat, which is a far more accurate measure. In fact, I carry around a portable ultrasound, a device that connects to my laptop and directly measures the layers of fat under the skin. It is accurate up to within a percentage point or so, and I use it to measure people's percentage body fat on request.

We lose muscle mass naturally as we age; this is the reason we put on weight and gain fat as we age. If we eat the same amount of food but exercise less, the muscle mass will slowly waste away, and will be replaced by fat. This is so simple to understand. Muscles must be exercised in order to maintain their mass and strength, so the main point of exercise is to build or maintain muscle. If you do not do this, you will get fat and put on weight, even if you eat the same amount as before.

If you lower the amount of food you eat to compensate for lack of exercise, you may not gain weight, but you may still get fat because your muscles shrink and you put on fat instead.

The maths can be complicated but it works like this: 5 lb of muscle, even in a state of rest, burns a total of 30–50 calories a day more than 5 lb of fat, which is not really that many more calories (a few potato chips). But to maintain this muscle, you need to burn 300–500 calories in the gym every week. In other words, you burn a modest 80–120 calories a day more for every 5 lb more muscle than fat, even if your total weight is the same.

But now it gets crazy. Your muscle-to-fat ratio is not a constant; it depends on exercise. If you are not exercising at all, you will lose your muscle mass over time. If you are eating the same amount, you now have a daily 120-calorie surplus, which translates into adding roughly 10 lb of fat a year to your body weight.

It gets worse. The idle burn rate for fat is only two calories per pound every day, so if you continue to eat more calories than you need, for every 5 lb of muscle loss, you will continue to gain weight until you put on 50 lb of fat. Of course, this process will take five years or more, but you see the point I am making—obesity can simply result from failure to maintain muscle as we age.

When to Eat Whatever You Like

Do not be obsessed with food. Both positive obsessions (what should I eat?) and negative obsessions (what should I not eat?) are bad for you. Once in a while, you can eat whatever you like. The idea is that practising self-control 100 per cent of the time puts a limit on your freedom. Your mind will rebel against it. This is not what you want. It's okay to have a weekly cheat day. I tell my mentees that they should follow a cleansing diet strictly for twenty-one days (to show their commitment) where they avoid sugar and sugary carbs like rice and wheat and pasta. After that, they can enjoy a cheat day once a week, where they can eat anything they want. The idea is that once your body has stopped craving sugar, even on cheat days you are less likely to consume much of it. I have found this to be personally true. For the first six months I used to look forward to the Saturday cheat day. But now, I no longer even have a cheat day as I don't have those cravings. I just naturally eat healthy 90 per cent of the time.

In a year, assuming you eat three meals a day, you will eat nearly 1,100 meals, of which 1,000 may be good meals and 100 bad. This happens to the baby elephant too. Sometimes, the baby elephant stumbles on a stash of fermented fruit. This is when she has a massive party with the rest of her herd. If you have never been to an elephant party, you sure are missing out on something. These parties are wild, and you have never seen revelry until you witness (from a safe distance) a herd of 3-ton elephants drinking and running around a forest or, worse, the high street in a village.[2] But luckily for elephants as well as the rest of the forest, this does not happen very often.

Humans are also social animals who like a varied diet. If we so habituate ourselves that we are eating 1,000 good, healthy meals in a year, it is perfectly okay, even a couple of times a week, to allow ourselves to eat whatever we want to eat. But do we truly know what a good meal is? I would say the vast majority of us have no idea what a healthy meal is and what is an unhealthy one. Even worse, most people, including doctors and nutritionists, have totally wrong notions, just like I did for many decades until my research opened my own eyes.

Just like those people who believe that the sun goes around the earth, we are labouring under huge misconceptions. To make matters worse, some food companies spread blatant misinformation by advertising their brand of sugary drink or namkeen snacks as 'healthy', and we find ourselves believing this utter nonsense.

2

Mumbo-Jumbo: The Elephant's Guide to All the Confusing Terms about Diet

Glycaemic Index and Calculations That Will Make Your Eyes Glaze Over

We are obsessed with measurements. We believe that if we can put some numbers together, we will be able to take control of our lives. Right? Actually, wrong! The easiest and best decisions in life do not involve numbers at all, but a simple and emotional connection to the world around us.

We will discuss this emotional connection with food in later sections of the book, but let me first introduce you to a fad called the glycaemic index (GI). This is a way of counting sugar that remains popular with many people today, especially people who have not succeeded in achieving their fitness and diet goals. In fact, I have not yet come across a fit person who gives a second thought to these metrics.

Can you imagine the baby elephant worrying about the GI of foods? The fact is that the GI only matters when you live in a world where 90 per cent of what you eat comes from a factory. If you don't eat processed food, which the baby elephant most certainly does not, you don't have to worry about the GI. But sadly, most of us do eat a lot of processed junk. So it is worth exploring what the GI is and why it matters.

Simply put, the GI is a number between 1 and 100. Low is good, high is bad. Glucose is 100, which is basically pure sugar.

People who eat high-glycaemic foods are more likely to be obese and develop diseases like diabetes, heart disease, high blood pressure, thyroid problems and cancer. This is because of a simple truth: sugar is poison.

If you eat high-glycaemic foods, your body produces a lot of insulin to counter the sugar spike in your blood. Over time, this will cause insulin resistance. What this means is that insulin loses its ability to counter sugar inflammation. A leading heart surgeon has described excess sugar as 'liquid sandpaper' in your blood, causing abrasion and inflammation everywhere it goes.

But not all sugar is the same, which is why we need to understand the concept of GI. For example, an orange is a perfectly healthy part of our diet, with a low GI, wonderful fresh taste and lots of vitamin C. But on the other hand, orange juice has a very high GI. What's the difference? The main difference is fibre. When you remove fibre from food that contains sugar, its GI shoots up. What is otherwise a very healthy food can become toxic and highly damaging without fibre. This is the reason store-bought juices are bad for you. When you drink juice, you feel good for all the wrong reasons—juices are packed with sugar that is easily absorbed by your body, which is why they give you a quick sugar high. Your sugar high is followed by a sugar crash, and then you go looking for more sugar. Don't fall into this trap. We will discuss more about fibre in later chapters, because fibre is really the hidden health secret in the Baby Elephant Diet.

Did you know there is a simple way of converting a high-glycaemic food into a low-glycaemic food?

Before I tell you what the answer is, just bear with me for a moment. This book is all about fibre, that essential quality of food that keeps us healthy precisely because it is inert and passes through the body. For those of you who remember your chemistry lessons, you might recall that there are substances called catalysts, which do not by themselves take part in chemical reactions but speed them up when you add them. Fibre works the opposite way. By slowing down the absorption of sugar, and making your body consume more energy to process your food, fibre actually becomes a catalyst for good health. If you are dependent on carbohydrates for most of your calorie intake—as people who follow the normal Indian diet or SAD are—fibre becomes the key ingredient in weight management.

Let us logically think of what the GI is. It is simply the ability of a food to be turned into sugar and absorbed by your body. The higher the GI, the higher the sugar absorption rate, and the faster you will get fat, or diabetic, or probably both. High blood pressure, thyroid problems, chronic stress, sleep disorders, skin ailments, these are all caused by eating high-glycaemic foods. But we know that most foods in their fibre-laden form have a low GI, and in their juice form a high GI. For example, oranges are healthy whereas orange juice, according to me, is a sugar-laden poison (all juices, in fact, are the same) that one should never consume after the age of 30. There is a popular brand of orange juice sold in India that has more added sugar than colas. The difference between an orange and orange juice is simply fibre.

The reality is that most of us do not have the time or the inclination to look at the GI of foods. Instead, I recommend a very simple checklist. If a food item comes in a box, it probably has a high GI. If it is a sweet liquid or if it is semi-solid, it probably has a very high GI. Fruits and vegetables are generally okay, but avoid bananas, grapes, apples, mangoes; these are especially sugary in India. Potato is not a vegetable, it is a sugar bomb. Of course, the baby elephant loves bananas, but as we will see later in this book, the bananas found in the wild have no resemblance to the hybrid, commercially grown sugar-laden fruit available to us.

So if juicing a health food turns it into a sugar bomb, then, logically, the opposite must be true, right? Well, sort of. There is, indeed, a way of lowering the GI of a food, and the answer to the question at the top of this section is, '*Don't chew your food.*' If you swallow food without chewing, it automatically lowers its GI, because, after all, chewing is nothing but mechanically pulping something and adding mouth enzymes and saliva to it. There was, in fact, a fad diet in the late 1970s that was briefly popular, encouraging people not to chew their food in order to lose weight.

Now I want to make one thing clear. *I would never ever recommend such a diet.* I am merely using this old fad to illustrate the point that foods have intrinsic qualities that depend also on how you consume them. An orange is in no way the same substance as a glass of orange juice, even if it is freshly squeezed.

On the contrary, chewing well is highly recommended by ancient and modern wisdom. In ayurveda, chewing each morsel eighteen times is recommended. The baby elephant definitely chews all its food. The whole process of mastication, where we release the nutrients in the food and soak them in saliva and mouth enzymes, is highly beneficial. For starters, it consumes energy to chew. Second, the enzymes are very helpful in signalling the stomach to produce acid and in kick-starting the digestion process. And last but not least, chewing releases the flavours on to our taste buds so we enjoy the food more. Please note that I am a food lover. Fresh, tasty food can add immensely to the joy of living, and everything I say in this book is meant to preserve this other essential quality of food. Food is meant not just for the body, it also nourishes the soul. I go to great lengths to obtain and enjoy fresh food with varied ingredients. We will see in a later section how that quest is inherently compatible with conservation, sustainability and a love of nature.

Nothing beats eating fresh, natural food that has essential fibre in it. This is what we humans have evolved to eat, and this is what keeps our bodies and our bacterial ecosystems healthy and fit.

Learning from Your Enemy: What the Sugar Industry Inadvertently Teaches You

Raju eats at the vegetarian Udupi hotel every day. He orders a thali, which is a large plate with small bowls of vegetables and dal, accompanied by some yogurt (curd), papad and dessert. You can order an unlimited amount of rice and sambhar. Raju binges on the rice every time he visits the Udupi hotel, mixing the vegetables with the rice in a big heap and devouring it. Raju is 35 years old and already obese and pre-diabetic.

It is extraordinary that all the healthy foods in this restaurant are served in small bowls, while the unhealthy rice is served in unlimited quantities. We mix the healthy foods into heaps of rice (which is nothing but pure sugar), and then eat this concoction. When you look at a bowl of rice, do you realize that it is nothing but sugar?

Let me explain this in detail. Each rice molecule is essentially two sugar molecules, one of glucose and one of sucrose (white rice also has 7 per cent protein, so it is actually technically 93 per cent sugar).

One way of measuring the impact of the food we eat on our blood sugar is the GI. The closer the number is to 100, the closer the food is to pure glucose. Glycaemic load (GL) refers to the amount of sugar available in a given food. This is, of course, influenced by portion size, so I don't pay a lot of attention to it.

As the table on page 24, sourced from a sugar industry website,[3] inadvertently points out, these are all the known poisons in our diet (although the sugar industry obviously does not say that).

This table (again inadvertently) pretty much lists all the food that we should cut out of our lives. The baby elephant does not eat any of these foods (well maybe an occasional carrot and an occasional apple are okay). The sugar poison manufacturers want us to see this chart and think, 'Ah, carrots are more sugary than sugar, so sugar is okay.' First of all, the number attributed to carrots is a lie, pure and simple (the real number is around 40, according to many other sources), there just to mislead the public. Second, the rest of the junk in this chart is not something the baby elephant would find in the wild.

Comparison of GI and GL of certain foods

Food	GI	Glycemic (GL)
Apple	40	6
Baked potato	85	26
Brown rice	50	16
Carrots	92	5
Corn flakes	92	24
Orange juice	50	13
Plain bagel	72	25
Potato chips	54	11
Pound cake	54	15
Wheat bread	53	11
Table sugar (sucrose)	58	6

Why Virat Kohli Can Drink That Sugary Cola and Stay Fit (but You Can't)

Have you seen cola advertisements on TV? Indian batting sensation Virat Kohli leans back, takes a swig of a dark sugary carbonated drink and smiles, seemingly refreshed. The message is simple. Drink the cola and you will be successful in sports like Kohli.

A can of this witches' brew otherwise called cola, has 41

gm of pure sugar—which is about ten teaspoons of sugar—a lot of caffeine and carbonated water. If a person weighing 80 kg were to run up a flight of steps, can you guess how many floors he would have to run (not walk) up to burn off a can of cola? The answer is around thirty-five floors, that is assuming he runs up the thirty-five-floor building in eight minutes. If he runs at a slower pace than that, he will need to climb up even more floors. The same person weighing 80 kg, will take thirty-five minutes of normal walking to burn off the cola drink. So if you are in the habit of running up buildings, go ahead and gulp down that can.

Virat Kohli has several advantages that you and I likely do not. For one thing, he is a young man aged twenty-four, and his metabolism is a lot faster than that of an older person. Metabolism is measured with the basal metabolic rate (BMR). Your BMR depends on your age (the older you are, the lower the BMR), muscle mass (the less the muscle, the lower the BMR), stress levels (high stress lowers BMR), sleep (if you are not getting enough sleep, BMR goes down) and cardio fitness (if you are less fit, BMR goes down). Virat Kohli can eat around eighty calories a day more than an equally fit thirty-four-year old can, or 160 calories a day more than a fit forty-four-year old, or 240 calories a day more than a fit fifty-four-year old. Essentially, the difference between someone Virat's age and me is that he can have one can of cola more than I can every day, even if I were as fit as he is.

The second thing, of course, is that Virat is a professional sportsman. Assuming he works out three hours each day at the gym and in fielding drills, he is burning 1,500 calories a day more than someone his own age who is not a sportsman.

A can of cola a day, or even two cans, is not going to make much difference to an elite athlete or professional sportsman.

But what does cola do to the rest of us mortals? Well, there are about 8,800 calories in 1 kg of human fat, so basically if you drink two cans of cola a day on top of your normal food intake, you will gain 1 kg of fat every month.

This is a classic example of the lies we are told by the sugar industry. Kohli gets over Rs ten crore per endorsement, so you can't blame him for peddling these products. But think of the enormous harm caused by the sugar products industry to the Indian public. These sugar products not only turn into fat in our bodies, but they also cause diabetes, high blood pressure, heart disease, stroke and cancer. Moreover, products that are harmless when you consume them once in a while, become deadly when you consume them regularly, which is what the sugar-products industry aims at achieving through its advertising blitzkriegs. They affect the quality of your life in later years and are a huge public health menace.

What about children? Of course their metabolism can handle the occasional cola product, but why would you want them to develop a positive association or a taste for something that is so harmful later in life? Get them used to eating healthy foods instead.

The solution at a policy level is not difficult. We simply look at the overall damage caused by the cola industry to public health, and make it set aside profits that can be used when needed, like an insurance policy. This is similar to the tobacco industry settlements that happened in the US. In the meantime, you can do your bit. Never touch the stuff. Never let your children touch the stuff.

The best habit you can inculcate in your children is regularly drinking plain water. Once they develop a taste for water, it will stay with them for the rest of their lives. You will be surprised at how many privileged children these days think that they don't need to drink water and can live on soda or juices or milk alone. Don't make that mistake in your home. There is also no reason to drink any of the fancy 'waters' doing the rounds, such as vitamin-added water, oxygenated water and whatever other current health-fad water there is. It's all factory-made marketing junk. Save your money and fill up from the filtered water tap at home.

I want to make an additional point about sugar. You would probably be astonished to know the truth about one of the most popular brands of orange juice in India—a brand that I cannot actually name in a book, but think of something that advertises itself as 'genuine orange juice'. This juice actually contains more sugar than a cola drink in the same quantity. The company openly advertises the product as orange juice, but it is nothing but sugar syrup masquerading as juice.

Is Rice Really That Bad?

One of the main culprits behind the Indian vegetarian's descent into diabetes is undoubtedly rice. And yet, the Japanese eat a fair amount of rice and they are the healthiest and longest-living people. How is this possible?

This is not a question that has a clear-cut answer based on the available science. A simple explanation could be that north Asians have simply evolved to be able to eat rice without significant ill-effects. It could also be that they do not eat other forms of sugar at all (no sweet tooth), so their overall carbohydrate consumption is lower. It could well be that there is an inverse relationship between lactose tolerance (most north Asians are lactose intolerant and cannot have dairy) and rice tolerance. In other words, people who cannot digest milk may have a better ability to process rice without developing insulin resistance.

A top fitness trainer in Singapore once showed me how to measure whether we have the ability to eat rice (without causing damage) or not. He simply measured the fat under my shoulder blade using calipers. Apparently, the less fat there is, the more rice you are able to eat. He was right; I do have the ability to eat more rice without gaining body fat. But then again, I am also lactose intolerant so this fits in with my earlier hypothesis.

The point is that rice has been a staple food in north Asian diets for centuries, whereas it is very new to South Asian diets. Despite what people believe in India, rice was rarely available in India until the 1920s. Even in south India, ragi or millet was the staple food at that time, and rice was prohibitively expensive and out of reach. This changed after the arrival of Sir Arthur Cotton in south India in the 1920s. He built the dams on the big southern rivers, the Cauvery, the Kollidam and the Godavari, that turned the flood plains of the south into a rice bowl. This made rice plentiful and cheap, and it very quickly replaced millet as a staple. As a result, there has been an upsurge of diabetes in India. There is no doubt that reducing the quantity of or removing rice from the Indian diet as we get older will dramatically reduce our risk of diabetes. Most rice eaters consume far too much of it. Please understand that white rice is 93 per cent sugar. If you consider how much rice people eat at one sitting, you will understand why we are facing an epidemic of heart disease and diabetes.

The Tale of the Poison-filled Cupboard, and Aunty Sunita's Blind Spot

My dear aunt Sunita emailed me recently. 'Ravi, I have been following the 'Baby Elephant Diet' and lifestyle religiously, but I haven't lost much weight.' I was intrigued, because I now have over a hundred people following my diet, and the results are excellent. It was time for a forensic investigation at Aunty Sunita's home.

On a sunny Sunday afternoon, I knocked at her door. 'Helloooo!' said a familiar sing-song voice and Aunty Sunita appeared with her million-watt smile. But I could see what she meant when she said that my diet was not working. She was as rotund as ever, looking like the most eligible bachelorette in Uganda.[4] In Uganda, there is marked preference for obese spouses in the villages, so much so that girls are literally fattened up by their relatives before they are married off. This is because for historic reasons, being fat is associated with being wealthy and healthy. But of course, Aunty Sunita was not about to become a Ugandan bride anytime soon!

After the pleasantries, I made a beeline for her kitchen to see what Aunty Sunita had in her refrigerator. It was full of fresh vegetables, whole milk, cheese, dark chocolate (85 per cent cocoa), paneer, eggs, mayo, butter , and not a single carton of juice…so far an A+ from me. The freezer was stocked with fish and frozen chicken…no problem there. Next I looked in the kitchen cabinets—there was no sign of cereal, rice, pasta, flour, sugar, honey. I was starting to worry… *How could Aunty Sunita be putting on weight with a kitchen stocked with healthy foods?*

'So Aunty, tell me what you have been doing since you started my diet' I asked, wondering if she was simply eating out all the time.

'Not much, son! I have been staying at home. You can't really eat out in India because the vegetarian food in restaurants is full of sugar carbs.'

Now I was flummoxed. Was she that rare individual who is unable to lose fat no matter what she eats?

As I was trying to work through this problem, the doorbell rang. 'Oh, it is my mahjong group,' said Aunty Sunita as she waddled to the door and let in four other aunties who were all plus-sized.

'You are the average of the five people you spend the most time with…'[5] this Jim Rohn quote danced in my mind's eye as I looked at the kitchen table, now occupied by this gaggle of famine-proofed aunties.

'Son, this is how I spend my afternoons these days. We meet mainly at my place for mahjong and a little gossip,' Aunty Sunita smiled at me.

I feared that the end of my investigation was near. I went to the living room and browsed through the daily papers, lost deep in thought, until the familiar 'tea time' call from my aunt's cook came an hour later. I walked back into the kitchen/dining area, and there it was on the table, a whole spread of potato samosas, flour murukus, potato and paapdi chaat, rice crackers, corn chips and dips.

'Aunty, what is all this?' I asked, aghast.

'This is just for when I have guests, son!'

'But you have guests every day for mahjong.'

'Yes son, but it is only at tea time,' my dear aunt smiled as she tucked into a fried samosa.

'But where do you keep all this stuff? I didn't see any of it in the kitchen,' I said.

'Oh it's not for me, so I keep it in the guest cupboard,' she pointed to the dining room cupboard, which was clearly marked 'guest cupboard'.

As I left Aunty Sunita's house, I marvelled at the power of sugar addiction. It is no different from addiction to alcohol or any other drug. Once you develop a dependency, the addiction will create a delusion that you don't have a behaviour problem and that whatever symptoms you are experiencing are beyond your control, i.e. they are genetic.

Here was my aunt, a perfectly sane and reasonable person, who simply put all her junk food into a cupboard marked 'guest'. She ate healthy food three times a day but consumed at least 1000 calories of sugar from the 'guest' cupboard daily while entertaining her mahjong group. She was by no means the fattest of her mahjong group, so she never felt out of place when she was in their company.

Breaking sugar addiction can be challenging for some people, as difficult as quitting smoking, while other people do it with ease. We have to sympathize with our sugar-addicted loved ones, be patient with them, and ultimately respect their choices. But it is not impossible to break sugar addiction.

Aunty Sunita, I will find a way to rid your home of the poison cupboard…eventually!

The Two-word Mantra That Will Improve Your Health Forever

Very few things can be simplified into two words. This is especially true in the vast and complicated field of health. In the US alone some 12 per cent of GDP, or $1.5 trillion, each year is spent on healthcare. Can you imagine if someone came up with a two-word health formula that could shave at least 50 per cent off this enormous cost? How should a grateful society reward this person? Give them a billion-dollar reward? The Nobel Prize for medicine, at the very least?

So what is this magic formula?

Avoid sugar.

That's it. This is the secret of good health. If you can change your diet to avoid sugar in all its myriad forms, ranging from ice-cream to sodas, rice, pasta, wheat, bread, cereals, fruit juices and sweet fruits, you will live a long and healthy life. Sugar is the most inflammatory substance that is widely consumed in the world. Forget worrying about monosodium glutamate (MSG), saturated fat, trans fat, and cholesterol, forget the bogus calorie- restriction diets, forget the X number of small meals a day diet and forget the vegetarian versus non-vegetarian debate. These are all irrelevant in the great battle for improving human health. The only thing that matters is sugar and whether you can lower your consumption of it by 70-90 per cent. How do you know you are avoiding sugar? It's very simple. Just look in the mirror. If your body fat is 18 per cent or less if you are a man, and 25 per cent or less if you are a woman, you are avoiding sugar (or you are an elite athlete).

Think about the ramifications of what I just said. The biggest spenders of advertising dollars are the two big sugary drinks companies. Yes, a can of cola has, count 'em, twelve teaspoons of sugar in it. These companies claim to sell healthy drinks, but the reality is that the vast majority of their sales come from liquid sugar. How different are these companies from those selling tobacco, as far as public health is concerned? And yet they are allowed to market not just to adults but also to children. There is a clear market failure here. The solution will have to take many forms, but we can start by ratcheting up the taxes on sugar and sugar products, and using the money to pay for educating people on the dangers of sugar.

Diabetes and Its Nasty Friends

Let me explain in simple terms what type 2 diabetes is, and how to prevent it and reverse it. Diabetes is a metabolic illness, meaning that it is caused by your own body and not a disease agent. In normal people, blood sugar is controlled by a hormone called insulin. In diabetic people, insulin no longer does its job because the body develops resistance to it. This causes blood sugar levels to remain at high levels.

Here is the crux: 90 per cent of the health problems among non-smokers in the developed world are a direct result of too much dietary sugar (and its associated carbs, namely rice, pasta, wheat and potatoes).[6]

The other day someone said to me, 'My mother-in-law has diabetes but she is rail-thin, even underweight. How is this possible?'

Here is how this is possible. Eating excess sugar and fast carbs leads to:

1. Excess body fat
2. Diabetes
3. Heart disease
4. High blood pressure
5. Stroke

If you have a sugary diet, you can get any one, or all five, of these illnesses. It is true that most people with diabetes are overweight or have excess body fat, but the real culprit is the ongoing sugar intake, not the body fat. So underweight people who live on a sugar and fast-carbs diet can also develop diabetes.

If you are obese and you eliminate sugar, you will drop body fat and become healthier. If you look skinny to begin with, you can still benefit from cutting down on the fast carbs. You can always control or reverse type 2 diabetes, and lower your heart disease risk and stroke risk just from eliminating sugar (even if you don't drop body fat).

Here is my bonus theory on sugar and nicotine addiction

Have you ever wondered why smokers are often skinnier than non-smokers? It is because they are addicted to nicotine. Nicotine and sugar are both highly addictive substances, but being addicted to one provides a kind of immunity from being addicted to the other at the same time. This is also the reason why people gain weight when they stop smoking; many unwittingly replace the nicotine addiction with a sugar addiction.

Don't Drink Your Calories: Why Drinking Orange Juice Can Lead to Diabetes

Before I address the link between orange juice and diabetes, I want you to think about a more basic question. How do humans eat? Let us explore this in a logical way, because if you know what happens to the food you eat, you can take simple measures that will help you lose excess fat.

First we cook food

Humans learned how to cook food around 50,000 years ago. The three reasons cooking became popular are: (1) It kills pathogens. (2) It makes inedible food edible. (3) It makes food combinations that are tastier and make use of leftover scraps. However, it is important to know that increasing the amount of raw food we eat, such as salads and low-sugar fruit, is better for losing weight because raw food is harder to break down and digest.

Next we put the food in our mouths

At this point, the food we eat is mostly not in a form that is digestible. If the food is a solid, we subject it to mechanical desiccation, otherwise known as chewing. While chewing, this food is also mixed with saliva, which contains enzymes that aid in digestion. The process of chewing consumes energy, which is why it is better to eat solid food than liquid food if you want to lose weight. Simply avoiding drinking your calories goes a long way in fat loss.

Then we swallow the food

This is the last manual or voluntary task we perform with food before the body's automatic process takes over. Swallowed food goes through your oesophageal sphincter into your stomach, where it is given a bath in stomach acid. The amount of stomach acid we produce depends on many factors, but generally speaking, people who are overweight tend to produce more stomach acid than skinny people. High stomach acid generally increases food absorption which can lead to obesity and type 2 diabetes.

The food gets an enzyme bath

The food gets bathed in enzymes and other secretions of the liver and pancreas.

The food slurry undergoes bacterial decomposition

The food slurry enters the intestines, which are a 25-foot-long tube, where it undergoes bacterial decomposition from the trillions of bacteria that live there. If you have ever seen how quickly bread flour rises when it is mixed with yeast and sugar, you will have a sense of what happens to the slurry when trillions of bacteria break it down. You essentially get a bacterial soup that is rapidly broken down into nutrients that are in a form easily absorbed by the lining of your gut. Any food that is still undigested will push the soup further down the intestinal tract.

The nutrients from the food are absorbed

As it is passing through the intestine, the dissolved sugar, fat, protein and other nutrients from the now digested food are absorbed into the bloodstream. This is the step at which food is essentially converted into energy.

The unabsorbed food mixed with excess bacteria is eliminated

At the very end of the journey, the undigested fibre in the food, plus a bacterial content of around 25 per cent, reaches the anus where it is expelled through a bowel movement.

This whole process operates like an assembly line in a factory, with food being converted into energy. What we should realize is that this is one factory where you should not increase the efficiency, because excess sugars that are absorbed by the body are converted by the liver into body fat. In fact, it is always better to eat foods that are harder to digest, such as vegetables, proteins and seed-filled fruits like guavas, instead of easily digestible sugars like rice, wheat and pasta.

This finally brings us to the problem of orange juice! Orange juice is a liquid, sugar-filled, fibreless and acidic concoction that violates every rule of the human digestive system. By totally short-circuiting the digestion process, orange juice basically makes itself and any food it meets in the stomach more easily digestible and more easily absorbed. It is essentially a catalyst for obesity, which, of course, is the main cause of type 2 diabetes.

There is a concept called metabolic resistance which we will explore later. People with high metabolic resistance are skinny, and those with low metabolic resistance are fat. Orange juice lowers your metabolic resistance and makes you fat. By all means eat an orange whenever you wish...but do not drink orange juice, freshly squeezed or store-bought, if you want to avoid diabetes. You can enjoy orange juice as an occasional treat, of course!

Why You Should Never Drink Low-fat Milk

Here is some information, followed by a simple question.

Full-fat milk has 145 calories in a cup, and fat-free milk has 85 calories per cup. Both have the same amount of sugar carbs—12 gm a cup.

What kind of milk should you choose, if you want to lose weight and be healthy? The answer is that you should always choose full-fat milk!

If you are one of those people who drink only skimmed or fat-free milk and believe that is healthier than full-fat milk, think again! If you drink fat-free milk, essentially you are drinking sugar water. Let me explain.

Protein aside, milk has sugar and fat. If you remove the fat, what do you end up with? That's right, sugar! Besides, with low-fat milk, you need to drink more of it to feel full and satisfied. It is far better for health to drink full-fat milk. You will feel full with a smaller serving, and, as a result, you will consume less sugar than if you were to have a larger serving of low-fat milk.

There are three reasons why people drink low-fat milk.

1. It is deeply ingrained in our minds that fat is bad for us. This is a completely false premise. Sugar is the culprit, not fat.
2. There is a perception that low-fat milk is cheaper. This is not really true.
3. Milk producers have encouraged us to drink low-fat milk. We will see the reason for this later in the Bonus Explanation!

'But what about the cholesterol?' people ask me all the time when I ask them to switch to full-fat milk. I challenge anyone to show me a single study that full-fat milk increases cholesterol. In fact, low-fat and non-fat milk are the real culprits in increasing cholesterol because they are essentially nothing but sugar water.

The irony is this. If you are truly a calorie counter, you should know that 200 calories of low-fat milk is far, far more fattening than 200 calories of full-fat milk. This is because the low-fat milk, which is entirely sugar, will spike your insulin and increase your cholesterol levels.

Low-fat and non-fat milk are a complete scam!

Here is another reason why you should drink full-fat milk, if you consume milk at all. The fat in milk is actually good for you. Many studies show that the essential nutrients in milk are almost entirely fat-soluble nutrients. If you remove the fat, you also remove the nutrients.[7] There are also studies that show that consuming high fat dairy products makes you actually lose weight and reduces your risk of heart disease and diabetes![8]

Please, for the sake of our health, let us start a campaign to rename fat-free milk as sugar-loaded milk. We can also rename whole milk as low-sugar milk. Of course, it is true that a glass of full-fat milk has more overall calories than a glass of fat-free milk. But who says you need to drink a big glass of milk? Just get a smaller glass and drink full-fat milk.

Bonus Explanation

If you have flown United Airlines recently, you will have seen that the airline has a new way of squeezing more money out of flyers. In the past, the economy class cabin used to have the same legroom for each seat. The bean counters at United (and some other airlines) have now figured out that if you take the same number of seats, but you arrange them so that the back section has no legroom at all, and the front section has more legroom, then people will pay more money for the front section, even though both sections have the same economy-class seats, food and service. This way, the airline makes more money from the same cabin and with the same number of seats. Do you see how this is a variation of the low-fat milk scam?

Why do milk companies want us to drink low-fat milk? The answer is simple. They love to remove the fat from milk, and sell it as expensive butter and cream. You can think of low-fat and fat-free milk as the useless by-products of the butter industry. If consumers knew the truth about fat-free milk and stopped drinking it, the butter industry would have to throw it away. Instead, it is sold to us as a healthy alternative to full-fat milk, when the opposite is true.

How to Lose Weight on a Diet of Twinkies and Doritos

And now I want to deliberately confuse you, dear readers, with an inspirational story.

A fella by the name of Mark Haub, a professor of nutrition at Kansas State University, set out to prove a point. For ten weeks, two-thirds of his calories came only from junk carbs, including Twinkies, Doritos and Oreos. The rest came from a protein shakes and some vegetables. But he carefully measured everything before he ate it, and limited his food intake to 1,800 calories a day, as against a requirement of 2,000 calories a day for a man of his height, weight and physical activity. The result? He lost 27 lb of weight over ten weeks.[9]

Why is this so difficult to understand? If you measure everything before you put it in your mouth, and consume 10 per cent fewer calories a day than your daily requirement, it absolutely does not matter what you eat; you will still drop weight and drop fat. This is the basic law of eating. Eat less, and lose weight. But can you imagine how many hunger cravings Mark Haub would have had with this approach. What about the insulin spike followed by the sugar downer and how his energy levels would have fluctuated before and after meals? Does anyone wish to live like this, with hunger pangs and massive sugar highs and downs?

The other major point that everyone missed in this study was how much muscle he lost in that 27-lb weight loss.

Losing weight does not mean becoming healthier if you lose muscle and not fat.

It is entirely possible that someone following this diet would end up far unhealthier at the end of it, even with the weight loss, if their body fat percentage went up because of the muscle loss. Looking thin is not the same as being thin. We humans come in all shapes and sizes, and what matters is the body fat percentage, which means that people with not much muscle mass can look thin but still have a high percentage of body fat. Our takeaway from Mark Haub should be something entirely different. It is that life is too short to measure calories and spend an excessive amount of time thinking about how much we are eating. What we should learn from Mark Haub's experiment is this: do not count calories, because you have only a slim chance (no pun intended!) of succeeding in your weight loss programme if you do so.

The diet that is most likely to succeed is one where you change the composition of what you eat permanently, and eat as much food as you like but are careful about the foods you choose to eat. This is the essence of the Baby Elephant Diet. The diet that is most likely to succeed is one where you eat a varied diet that is rich in taste and variety, and you really enjoy your dining experience.

The Human Health Dilemma: Vegetarian or Non-Vegetarian

Here is a simple truth, and I am not taking a religious or cultural view here. We are meant to be omnivores, physiologically speaking. No other species of animal can eat the variety of plants and animals that humans can. All the stuff you hear about how meat takes three days to digest is absolutely false. There is nothing that takes more than eight hours to digest, and even if there were such an edible substance, your body would expel it undigested. Your digestive system is like a conveyor belt where food keeps moving from mouth to stomach to intestine and finally out of the body, while it goes through a series of steps to extract the nutrients contained in it. If this conveyor belt stops, it spells trouble.

One easy way of analysing our physical make-up is to measure the length of our intestines. Generally speaking, herbivores have much longer intestines than carnivores. This is because meat is easier to digest and absorb, and thus needs less intestine length to pass through, compared to plant matter.

If you have any doubt about this, leave some meat and some vegetables on a windowsill and see what spoils first. Obviously the meat will spoil faster, because microbes can eat meat much quicker than they can eat vegetables. The same thing is true of our intestines, which after all have somewhere near 80 trillion bacteria in them.

Now we know that cow intestines are about 80 feet in length, whereas a tiger's intestines are only 18 feet. Humans, whose intestines are 25 feet long, are somewhere in the middle, which neatly confirms our status as omnivores, meaning that we can eat both plants and animals.

Look at the positive side of being an omnivore; humans can quite easily adapt to a wide range of diets. For the most part, what we eat is largely down to availability in our natural environment. The Inuit of Canada are known to eat mainly whale blubber, which gives them a 95 per cent fat content in their diet. At the other extreme, people who live on the island of Okinawa in Japan eat a diet largely made up of rice, vegetables and fish, with a total carbohydrate content of 90 per cent. The Paleo diet, involves eating lots of protein. In short, we can adapt to any reasonable diet as long as we have a sense of what keeps us healthy.

It is fair to say that human diets in all geographies are a product of the natural environment. People living in colder climates traditionally had few choices for food, and their food tended to be high in sugar and starch, e.g. potato, corn, root vegetables, gourds and cured meats. Spices were not always available, and when they were, they were worth their weight in gold. In tropical countries, you had a much wider variety of food to choose from. But food spoils quickly in hot climates, so practices like curing, pickling and spicing evolved to keep it from spoiling and to disguise the taste of spoilt food.

So now we have to ask the question, vegetarian or non-vegetarian? The answer is both simple and complicated. As far as your physical health is concerned, the answer is that it absolutely does not matter. Both vegetarians and non-vegetarians can lead perfectly healthy and meaningful lives, and no amount of pseudo-science will change the fact that your body was designed to eat either diet.

The issue is more of lifestyle, tradition, religious faith and ethics. Here things get complicated. The general benchmark in vegetarian ethics is that we take human levels of sentience and ability to feel pain, and work backwards down the food chain to come to a point where this sentience is so minimal or lacking that these creatures are closer to plants than to us.

Purely from an ethical point of view, there is a sort of consensus that it is okay to eat lower-order animals up to and including shellfish, e.g. prawns, lobsters, mussels, clams. When you enter the realm of the higher-order species, you cross a line that stops only at primates. In other words, if you eat goats, there is no ethical reason to not eat dogs, cats and whales. But as I said, it is complicated, because most people who would eat mutton would recoil at eating horse meat. Pigs are easily more intelligent than dogs, but humans eat pigs, and people in most cultures will not eat dog meat.

Ethics aside, the moment we talk about religious restrictions, a whole new dimension kicks in. How do you tell an orthodox Jain who walks with a white cloth covering her nose and mouth, and sweeps the ground in front of her, that her body is home to 90 trillion bacterial cells? Most of us would be surprised to learn that milk is produced by mammals from their sweat glands. Who came up with a Hindu vegetarian diet that says drinking pregnant cow sweat is perfectly permissible but eating eggs from chickens is not? Clearly it was someone who designed a diet over thousands of years of tradition and culture. I totally respect tradition and culture, but only so long as they do not blend with modern food in a way that has a detrimental effect on our health. If we have to modernize our diets out of necessity, then we have to amend our traditions and culture as well.

This is a book about your health, your nutrition and what you should eat for peak health. The ethics of food are beyond the scope of this book, so let me be very clear—you can have a nutritious and healthy diet whether you are vegetarian or non-vegetarian. But vegetarians have a tougher time of it because they don't get enough protein. If you insist on being a vegetarian, find a way of eating at least 3 gm of protein for every kilogram of your body weight every day.

The other issue for vegetarian food lovers is how to get a variety of tasty and interesting foods into their diet on a regular basis. In societies like India where a large portion of the population is lacto-vegetarian, this is easy because the demand creates a supply of an unending variety of vegetables and fruits. But when I moved to a predominantly factory-farmed meat culture like the US, I was in for a very rude shock, as you will see in the next section.

Mystery Solved: Why Fruits and Vegetables from a Monoculture Farm Have No Flavour

The first time I went to a grocery store after moving to the US, I literally jumped with joy at the opulence of it all. It was 1989, and six months before the fall of the Berlin wall. Having grown up in socialist India, I had never seen anything like the Safeway supermarket, an amazing symbol of American opulence. I danced down the wide aisles of the huge store and rode the supermarket trolley like it was a mini-scooter, admiring the extraordinary variety of every category of, er…stuff. Eighteen types of toothpaste, twenty types of yogurt, and an entire aisle dedicated to varieties of soda pop, wow! The fruits and vegetables were perfectly waxed and huge compared to the little discoloured specimens found in India. I marvelled as my host mother Marlene selected these enormous, beautiful tomatoes and white onions and a head of lettuce that was bigger than my own head. We went back home, and I helped her make a salad, and we sat down to eat. I bit into a slice of tomato, ready for the burst of fresh flavour.

And…nothing! I blinked. I ate another slice. Same result. The lettuce was also tasteless, like a watery bite of nothing. Deflated, I followed my host mother's suggestion and loaded up my salad with some sugary sweet honey mustard dressing. How is it that the wealthiest nation on the planet produces the worst-tasting vegetables and fruits?

The main reason is actually a scientific one. It turns out that fruits and vegetables that ripen more consistently are also flavourless. In the wild, tomatoes ripen inconsistently. In evolutionary terms, there is a natural selection process that favours this because inconsistent ripening allows the tomatoes a greater chance to be eaten by birds and animals, thereby allowing for their seeds to spread and germinate. However, there is a genetic mutation that allows uniform ripening that affects a percentage of tomatoes, and this genetic change also happens to make the tomatoes less nutritious and devoid of flavour.[10]

Now think about this. There are two broad categories of tomatoes. Type 1 is full of nutrition and flavour, but this type ripens inconsistently, and comes in all kinds of colours, shapes and textures. Type 2 looks perfectly shaped, is of uniform colour and ripens uniformly, but it also happens to have no flavour. If you were a big US grocery chain, even a purportedly organic one, which type of tomato would you stock?

If you guessed type 2, you would be right, and you would also solve the mystery of why this is true not only of tomatoes, but the vast majority of fruits and vegetables in the US which have no flavour and are less nutritious compared to fruits and vegetables found in, say, a much poorer country like India. It is also true that most American consumers have never really tasted flavourful fruits and vegetables and they don't know the difference. This largely explains why when Americans go abroad, to Italy or Japan or India, and taste real vegetables for the first time, it is a major eye-opener! And yet, these flavourless vegetables are now coming to India. The big seed companies want to encourage farmers to grow branded, uniform, monoculture seeds, and it is only a matter of time before we succumb to their marketing clout. If we are going to take a stand on this, we have to do it now.

Implications for Health

What happens when we eat these tasteless vegetables? Actually, the reality is that even flavourless vegetables and fruits are quite nutritious and good for you; if this were not the case, no grocery store would stock or sell them. The problem is both direct and indirect. When you are faced with a flavourless salad, you are likely to douse it with a sugary dressing to cover up the lack of taste. A tasty Mediterranean salad in Greece or Italy is eaten with a dash of healthy, fresh olive oil. The entire salad-dressing industry in the US is there to feed sugar to unsuspecting Americans who are eating flavourless vegetables. The Mediterranean diet works best in the Mediterranean region for a reason.

Indirectly, when healthy food is tasteless, our taste buds will simply guide us towards junk food like chips, sugary drinks and saturated fats, so instead of a tasteless salad, we end up preferring burgers and fries. The golden rule of public health is that we have to make healthy food taste good. Think how delicious a Mediterranean diet is. This diet is difficult to follow in the US because the same vegetables that are so appetising in Greece taste so bland in the US. There is a mountain of difference between freshly grated parmesan cheese, and the pre-packaged mass-market junk that passes for parmesan in US grocery stores. Unfortunately, this junk is now being imported to India, with Indians seemingly fascinated with anything American. Having spent fourteen years in the US, let me tell you that American food and American restaurants are unhealthy, and there is nothing special about them other than the profits they make for their owners.

The Solution

In many parts of the United States, CSA (community-supported agriculture) farms are available that provide fresh fruits and vegetables that are not industrially produced. Just type CSA and your hometown/county into an Internet search engine, and you will see them. For a few hundred dollars in America, you too can enjoy the freshest fruits and vegetables throughout the growing season, and your kids can go and pick fresh vegetables at these farms too. The fact is that in the US and increasingly in urban India, members of the middle class spend a very small amount of their income on food. Spend a bit more, and you can enjoy better quality food. Your body is a temple; it deserves the most flavourful and nutritious food you can comfortably afford. Let us commit to supporting community farms in India too, and prevent monoculture from setting the food agenda in our country.

Trust Me, Don't Trust Your Parents.

If you don't agree with the heading of this section, let me tell you the story of a little boy who was asked by his mother to guard her living quarters while she bathed inside. Now it turns out that this little boy had not yet met his father, a powerful god, who had been out wandering in the mountains and who in turn did not even know that his wife had given birth to a baby boy while he was away. So the father happened to return home right at that moment and saw this strange little boy guarding his wife's quarters. In a fit of anger, the god chopped off the little boy's head. Now this story has a happy ending because the god was Lord Shiva, the wife was the Goddess Parvathi, and the little boy was none other than the hero of this diet book, Lord Ganesha, the baby elephant who ended up with an elephant's head and became the darling of everyone.

So as Lord Ganesha will tell you with a mischievous smile, please do respect and honour your parents at every turn, but that doesn't mean you have to listen to them blindly. Even when they are gods they can make mistakes.

Your parents have given you a genetic blueprint, as well as the bacterial ecosystem that inhabits your gut and your skin. You are actually a product of not just their genetic blueprint, but also their bacteria, their food habits and the common space and environment that you share with them in the first part of your life.

Genes Are Not Destiny

The astonishing truth that scientists have recently discovered is that your genes don't make your destiny. What makes your destiny is the power of your habits. For example, Japanese people on traditional Japanese diets are among the healthiest people in the world, with an obesity rate of only 3 per cent. When scientists followed the lives of Japanese who had immigrated to the US directly or via Hawaii, they found some astonishing facts. Those who switched to the Hawaiian diet (which is somewhere between a US diet and the Japanese diet) experienced an immediate increase in diabetes, blood pressure and heart disease, but they were still healthier than Americans. Those who moved to the US and switched to a fully

American diet, became obese like 28 per cent of Americans, and prone to the same illnesses as other Americans, in just one generation.[11]

If you have exceptionally healthy parents and grandparents, look carefully at their food and exercise habits, and please do imitate them. But if your parents and grandparents are not healthy, or have chronic disease like diabetes, hypertension and heart disease, you need to act now. While we may think that we can change the habits of our loved ones, I can assure you that changing other peoples' habits is nearly impossible. Focus on your own self first, and change people through leading by your own example.

What most of us think of as genetic diseases are actually lifestyle diseases, as Japanese immigrants to the US will tell you. They had exceptionally healthy grandparents and ruined their own health through bad eating habits in one single generation.

But there is some good news.

What works in one direction also works in the other. In other words, in the same way that Japanese Americans ruined their health in one generation by switching to an American diet, we can all become much healthier by switching our diet, gradually over the next three months, to the Baby Elephant Diet. But be prepared to encounter an array of forces that will discourage you from your goal of becoming healthier. Let me summarize what you may be up against.

The cultural angle

'But we come from a family of rice-eaters,' your chubby aunt will protest as she attempts to serve you rice.

Solution: Do not eat it, not even one bite, because then

you will have lost. Make a thick ball of it and place it outside your plate. Politely explain to your aunt that rice causes diabetes.

The health angle

'But curd (yogurt) rice is good for health,' your old diabetic uncle will point out as he polishes off a plateful of it.

Solution: Eat the yogurt in a bowl. When you mix rice into something, you are taking a largely healthy food and adding a pile of sugar into it. When you eat rice mixed with fried potatoes...well, you are asking for trouble.

The economic angle

You order a cheap thali meal in a restaurant. It comes with unlimited rice.

Solution: Eat all the curries in the thali, but don't touch the rice. If the food is too spicy without the rice, find another place to eat.

The habitual angle

'But what can he eat if he quits rice,' laments the wife.

Solution: Buy more vegetables. Make more curries. Eat more full-fat yogurt. Eat cashew nuts/ groundnuts/almonds. Scientists have found that people who consume a significant portion of their calories from nuts live longer[12] and have fewer chronic diseases than people who do not.

The envy angle

Some people look at a healthy person and are envious. They will test your resolve and by tempting you with the worst type of junk food.

Solution: Cut these people out of your life, they are not worth it.

The ignorant

'But I don't have a sweet tooth at all,' says your diabetic aunt as she loads her plate with potato fry. 'It must be my genes.'

Solution: Explain firmly and carefully that the most sugary foods are rice, potatoes, wheat, pasta and cereal. Savoury sugar is just as bad as sweet sugar; actually it is worse because you don't think you are eating sugar…but you are.

Diabetes: No, It Is Not in Your Genes and You Can't Blame Your Parents!

Did you know that type 2 diabetes is a 100 per cent preventable and 100 per cent reversible lifestyle disease? It should be simply renamed for what it is, preventable obesity disease (POD). Now I told you earlier not to trust your parents when they give bad dietary advice. Now let me also tell you, do not blame your parents for POD. POD is not genetic. You get it when you make bad dietary choices in life.

POD/diabetes is a lifestyle disease because it is a purely voluntary illness that no one needs to get. If it weren't such a pernicious illness that causes blindness, deafness, heart disease, stroke, loss of sensation in limbs, and a whole host of degenerative conditions that can make your last stage of life a living hell, I would not worry about it as much as I do.

Yet, among my friends who are over forty, no one is especially concerned about it and it is almost seen as normal to be diabetic.

'It's in my genes,' says a friend.

'My whole family has it. I can't do anything about it,' says another.

Recently there was an article on the BBC website about the genetic link between diabetes and people of Asian, African and Caribbean descent. Essentially, 50 per cent of people from this ethnic background get diabetes by the time they are eighty years old. In the case of people of European descent, the number is 25 per cent. This article quotes Dr Nish Chaturvedi, who said, 'Genetics could not explain the difference in diabetes rates as there were similar levels of "risky genes" across all groups. There is something else that puts them at higher risk and we're not sure what that is.'[13]

One thing is clear from this study...there is no genetic case for diabetes. The fact is type 2 diabetes is directly correlated to excess body fat, particularly visceral fat that builds around the organs and the waist. This fat is directly caused by a diet filled with sugars and fast carbs. The main culprits are rice, wheat, pasta, fruit juices, and sugary drinks. There is a growing body of evidence that sugar is a highly addictive substance. When you give up or reduce your intake of sugars and fast carbs, you go through a three-week withdrawal process that includes symptoms like headaches, nausea, and low energy.

The problem is that people from Asia, Africa and the Caribbean are more prone to sugar addiction. This is not genetic but cultural. Most people do not realize that rice = sugar, and wheat = sugar. Just because something is not sweet does not mean it is not sugar. Let us together take a stand against POD!

3

Positive Eating: The Transition to a Healthy and Tasty Diet

The Basic Truth about Diet and the Human Body

Why are some people skinny and others fat? Why are some people able to eat copious amounts of food without any impact on their weight or health? Why does exercise make a significant difference in some people, while in others it doesn't seem to work at all? I am going to answer all these questions in this section, but first, let us use an analogy to understand what is going on.

Scientists who study gardening or farming have long understood the rules of plant growth. Plants will die without three basic things: water, sunlight and carbon dioxide. Of these three, carbon dioxide is always available to plants; sunlight too is more or less available during the day at the plant's will (assuming the plant is sitting out in the sun). Water, on the other hand, is quite variable, especially in rain-fed fields and forests. Wild plants and trees can go for weeks or even months without much water. When these same plants are drenched with water during the rainy season, they still mostly survive.

What is going on here?

For humans, replace CO_2 with oxygen, sunlight with water

and water with food, and you can see how the analogy works. Essentially, while the amount of oxygen and water that we need is non-negotiable, the number of calories we need to consume on a daily basis is quite flexible, meaning that an adult can consume between 1,600 and 3,000 calories a day based on their physical activity and metabolic rate. There is a hypothesis that after a basic minimum calorie intake, the extra calories we consume have a negative impact on lifespan and overall health.

Scientists have tried calorie-restriction diets in a wide variety of animals, including humans, with the idea that a low-calorie diet can dramatically extend your lifespan. The results have not been encouraging. However, it has been found that intermittent fasting, which means skipping a meal or two during the week, is really good for you. If interval training is the best way of building cardio health and fitness, then intermittent fasting could also do the same thing.

This in itself is a powerful argument against those nutritionists who say that we should eat several small meals a day. No mammal species actually gets to eat small meals throughout the day. In fact, most animals are lucky to get to eat even once a day.

So what do we do with this information? First of all, we have to detach ourselves from our clearly unhealthy relationship with food. Many of us are food addicts. We not only consume far too much food, we also tend to eat all the wrong kinds of food. The two are actually linked. I have never met anyone who binges on salads or vegetables. But I know lots of people who binge on sugar and sugary carbs. An addiction to sugar and sugary carbs not only makes you eat more food in general, it also packs a double punch because sugar carbs have up to fifteen times more calories than vegetables, for the same amount of weight.

So is it just a question of willpower? No, it is not. Scientists have discovered that to a great extent, our cravings and our relationship with food are determined by the type of microbes we have in our gut. Probably over 90 per cent of the bacteria that live in our body are inside our gut, and the gut microbe ecosystem, which has some 80 trillion cells, has a huge impact on our body type as well as our moods and cravings. In the near future, we will all have access to techniques that can quickly alter our gut microbe composition and dramatically improve our health and sense of well-being. But in the meantime, we have to use slower methods.

First, it is important to recognize that if you are obese or unable to control your sugar cravings, it probably means that your gut microbe balance is out of whack. Don't blame your genetics for obesity, blame your microbiome (you probably inherited much of your microbiome from your parents, so, yes, you can blame them for it).

Second, recognize that changing your microbiome is a process; it takes time. Take small steps that will change your gut for the better. There is a simple path to great health, but it won't happen overnight. It takes about three or four months of concerted effort but, after that, the changes are more or less permanent.

Third, understand that the reason most diets fail is that your willpower has only so much strength. When dealing with a microbiome that constantly influences your moods and your behaviour, it is exceedingly difficult to change yourself through willpower alone. You need a new strategy; harness your microbiome to become your friend, to work for you and not against you in this endeavour.

Fourth, please understand that the world is arrayed against you. People, especially in India, want to show you their love through food, and they will undermine your efforts by tempting you with junk or even try to embarrass you into eating more by loading your plate. Don't fall for this. What people give you to eat or put in your plate is up to them, but what you put into your mouth is entirely up to you. Don't be afraid to waste food. It is much better left on the plate than wreaking havoc inside your body. Your loved ones won't be the ones getting diabetes, heart disease and high blood pressure from you stuffing your face with sugary carbs and sweets.

The next section discusses how you can change your microbiome for the better, but the main clue is that it involves the Baby Elephant Diet.

The Four Food Groups

I know what you are expecting. Who can forget the ridiculous food pyramid issued by the United Stated Department of Agriculture (USDA) that you can see on page 59.

This outrageous lie was fed to an unsuspecting American public by their own Department of Agriculture, and, it turns out, was heavily influenced not by the Department of Health, but by food growers. One would imagine that a healthy eating guide would be issued by the Department of Health, but instead the champion of US factory farming gets to not only issue this pyramid, but to ship it around the world along with horrible American factory farm-products.

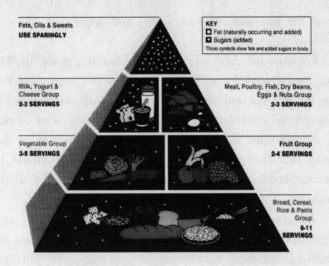

It is no wonder that after a few decades, the American public has started looking pyramid-shaped!

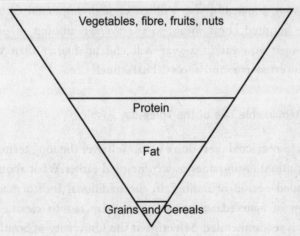

I use the inverted pyramid above, because frankly, I like the shape. Also, what you should be eating the most of should be at the top, and the junk sugars and cereals should be at the bottom.

For nine hundred meals a year, follow this guideline: The four food groups for an Indian should be two vegetables, two dals (or one dal and one meat/egg/fish dish), and a bowl of plain full-fat curd. You can sprinkle all these with a bit of rice.

Nutritionists and doctors often disagree with me on this, saying that the percentage of grains and cereals should be higher. Maybe that's true if you take the average of all the meals you consume in a year, but not on a daily basis.

The remaining hundred meals a year are your own; eat whatever you like. There will be weddings, funerals and birthdays, and there is tempting biryani, pizza, bhel puri and vada pav; as long as you follow my inverted pyramid for nine hundred meals a year, you can indulge guilt-free on special occasions. Inevitably, you will eat enough sugar and carbs in those hundred cheat meals, so the average amount of grains and sugar you eat in a year will end up higher than what this inverted pyramid shows. That's fine!

The Remarkable Tale of the Three-day Fast

Calorie-restricted diets don't work well over the long term, but intermittent fasting does, as we discussed earlier. What about an extended period of fasting? In the traditional Indian medical system of ayurveda, a one- to three-day fast to cleanse the body is recommended. Scientists at the University of Southern California found this ayurvedic practice to be beneficial,[14] in a recent experiment. They found that prolonged fasting activates stem cells of the immune system from a dormant state to a state of self-renewal. It is too early for Western medicine to recommend this three-day fast, but given the experiment confirms what Ayurveda has been saying for centuries, this might be a good method to try if you are suffering from any immune illnesses. As long as you drink water, you can easily go without food for three days. But do it under the supervision of a medical professional.

You Can Have a Bollywood Star's Body: The Definitive Guide to Losing Fat

Let me now go over the cruelly wrong advice that is otherwise known as the USDA food pyramid (see on page 59), promoted by the US Department of Agriculture since 1992. For nearly twenty years, the US government effectively promoted a diet that asked people to eat more carbohydrates, including bread, rice, cereals and pasta.

During this time, I was personally a victim of this diet. My body fat percentage was around 23 per cent for this entire twenty-year period because I followed the advice given in this food pyramid above. Chances are, you are also a victim of this food pyramid, and your body fat percentage is also well above 20 per cent.

In 2011, the USDA replaced this pyramid with something called ChooseMyPlate (see on page 62).

These people simply don't get it. If choosemyplate looks like it was put together by lobbyists for the dairy industry, the fruit industry and the cereals industry, that's because it was! It is astonishing that health and diet recommendations can be put together by vested food industry interests.

THIS IS ALSO BAD FOR YOU!

The Harvard School of Public Health has somewhat better advice in its Healthy Eating Plate:

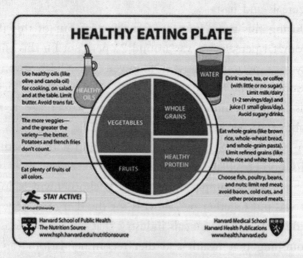

STILL BAD BECAUSE IT WILL NOT LOWER YOUR BODY FAT!

But here is the problem. For the 95 per cent of the population that has body fat of over 20 per cent (men) and 25 per cent (women), we need radical action to first bring the body fat percentages down to below 18 per cent (men) and 25 per cent (women). The Harvard plate above is more of a maintenance diet, but it will not get you to those body fat percentages.

I present to you the Baby Elephant Diet food chart, which is actually two charts. The first one is applicable for Sunday through Friday, and the second is a special one for Saturday only.

RAVIONHEALTH FOOD CHART FOR SUNDAY – FRIDAY

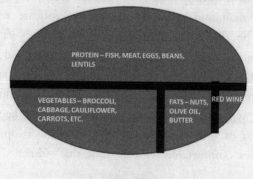

SATURDAY

What exactly is the Baby Elephant Diet lifestyle? It is nothing new or unique. It is simply a way of eating that has worked for me, and if you follow it, it will work for you too. I do not call it a mere diet, I call it a lifestyle and a paradigm shift. Once you start this lifestyle, you will never feel the desire to stop it. It is not something you follow for a few weeks or months and then go back to your old habits, because this way of eating will be satisfying and healthy, and most of all you will get results very quickly.

The Baby Elephant Diet lifestyle is an outcome-based approach to lowering your body fat to below 18 per cent if you are a man, and below 25 per cent if you are a woman. You will be able to achieve these levels of body fat if you follow this eating plan over the next few months, and by then your food habits would have permanently changed and your sugar cravings would be considerably reduced. With this eating plan, you will not only drop your body fat but keep it off for the rest of your life. Oh, and the red wine is optional. If you are not comfortable with alcohol, that's fine.

The Story of Fibre, or Why the Stuff That Passes Right through Our Body Is So Important

The baby elephant eats food that has 94 per cent fibre content, and fibre is the single most important ingredient in our diet that we never think about. It is a scientific fact that what passes through our body undigested is just as important as the nutrition that is actually absorbed by our body. Fibre comes only from plants, which is why eating a variety of plant-sourced foods, i.e. fruits, vegetables, nuts, shoots, leaves, is so essential for good health. Of course, as omnivorous humans we don't need to eat excessive fibre, but the point here is that modern diets are generally short on fibre, and most of us need to increase the fibre in our diet. A large number of diseases could be prevented by increasing the amount of fibre we eat.

Here is what you need to know about fibre: there are two kinds of fibre, water soluble and water insoluble. Soluble fibre is important because it reduces bad cholesterol and inflammation, and it regulates sugar intake. Soluble fibre binds with fatty acids in your stomach, slows down the time it takes to empty the stomach and lowers the rate of sugar absorption by the body. When you increase your soluble-fibre intake, you feel full longer, and you are less likely to go and look for snacks. When you eat this type of fibre, it goes through the digestive tract and is fermented by bacteria. It absorbs water, and becomes gelatinous, making for a smooth passage through your intestines.

Soluble fibre also plays a big role in keeping the bacteria in your gut healthy. A healthy gut bacteria ecosystem is the single most important criterion for a disease-free and long life. People who eat lots of soluble fibre are actually less likely to be fat and much less likely to suffer from immune illnesses or vitamin and mineral deficiencies. Natural food has the highest amount of soluble fibre. It is virtually non-existent in processed food. So if you choose foods with soluble fibre, you will end up making healthier choices. The table on page 66 shows the amount of fibre in some common foods:

Cereal Grains (½ cup cooked)	Soluble	Insoluble
Barley	1gm	4gm
Oatmeal	1gm	2gm
Oat Bran	1gm	3gm
Fruit (medium-size)	**Soluble**	**Insoluble**
Apple	1gm	4gm
Banana	1gm	3gm
Blackberries (½ cup)	1gm	4gm
Orange	2gm	2-3gm
Nectarine	1gm	2gm
Peach	1gm	2gm
Pear	2gm	4gm
Plum	1gm	1.5gm
Prunes (¼ cup)	1.5gm	3gm
Beans (half cup, cooked)	**Soluble**	**Insoluble**
Black beans	2gm	5.5gm
Kidney beans	3gm	6gm
Lima beans	3.5gm	6.5gm
Navy beans	2gm	6gm
Northern beans	1.5gm	5.5gm
Pinto beans	2gm	7gm
Lentils	1gm	8gm
Chick peas	1gm	6gm
Black-eyed peas	1gm	5.5gm
Vegetables (half cup, cooked)	**Soluble**	**Insoluble**
Broccoli	1gm	1.5gm
Brussels sprouts	3gm	4.5gm
Carrots	1gm	2.5gm

Insoluble fibre is found in the skins of vegetables and fruit and the bran portion of grains. Insoluble fibre helps promote regularity and a healthy digestive system. Insoluble fibre has many functions, including moving bulk through the digestive tract and controlling acidity levels in the intestines. It promotes regular bowel movement, prevents constipation and speeds up the elimination of toxic waste through the colon. By regulating the acidity in the intestines, insoluble fibre helps prevent microbes from producing substances which can lead to colorectal cancer.

Fibre has been found to lower the risk of stroke,[15] lower the risk of death[16] and cure asthma.[17] Stunningly, we now have evidence that fibre can indirectly regulate blood pressure because it promotes the growth of gut bacteria that have a positive impact on blood pressure.[18] One of the most credible research studies that was carried out from 1984 to 1996, called the 'Nurses Study', looked at the dietary habits of 74,000 nurses in the US. It found a clear link between a low-fibre diet and obesity.[19]

Think about this for a moment. Constipation is caused by lack of fibre in the diet. Irritable bowel, colitis, piles—these are all due to lack of fibre. Given that fibre is all important for health, why is it that fibre consumption has decreased so much these past few decades? The answer is simple: fibre consumption has decreased because of the processed food industry. Consider how much fibre there is in a fast food meal consisting of a burger, fries and a cola (the answer: almost none), or in processed foods like namkeen, juices, sweets (again, the answer is none). This is the problem. Stop focusing on calories and stop trying to remove fat from your diet. All you need to do is focus on increasing the fibre you eat at every meal, and all the other problems with your diet will be automatically addressed. You will not eat namkeen because it has no fibre. You will not drink your calories in the form of juices or colas because these have no fibre.

Idlis are out, white rice is out, bread is out, chapathis are out—these are all foods with hardly any fibre. The point is that you are causing serious damage to your body by eating foods with minimal fibre. Junk food is easier to digest, so a body fed on junk food will not only get obese, it will also lose its natural ability to eat a nutritious and fibre-rich diet. Some people complain that they get gas when they eat beans or cabbage or lentils. The reason is that they have altered their gut bacterial composition and their body has become weaker owing to their junk food addiction, so when they eat natural food, their body's initial reaction is negative. It takes a sustained period of eating vegetables to restore the body's ability to digest and process healthy food again.

If you were to organize your food intake in terms of priority, it would be fibre first, protein next, fat third and carbohydrate/sugar last.

Unfortunately, in today's world, the opposite is true. People eat far too many carbs, and consume far too much of unhealthy oils. They eat too little protein and far too little fibre. This is the real reason for the epidemic of chronic, immune diseases like diabetes, heart ailments and high blood pressure.

When you wake up in the morning, look for a source of fibre first, like guava, papaya or pomegranate. Eat some protein next, like eggs. If you eat the egg yellow, you will also get some good fats and amino acids. Have a few nuts like cashews or almonds to get both protein and some good fats. Have a cup of dal or millet if you are still hungry.

Fibre, an essential part of the Baby Elephant Diet, is Lord Ganesha's staple. So make fibre your new diet mantra. Make a pact with Lord Ganesha and promise yourself that you will choose to eat all his favourite foods, and you will see positive results within a month.

A Word of Warning about Fibre

Having read this book and impressed with its science, you want to make immediate changes to your lifestyle. So you rush to the fruit vendor, buy 2 kg of guavas, come home and eat about half a kilo of them.

What do you think will happen?

You will get a stomach ache and possibly bloating, cramps and gas. You will curse me, and promptly go back to your sugary cola drink, which will probably make you feel better by settling your stomach.

Please don't do this.

Your body needs time to adjust to any new diet. Doctors recommend around 40 gm of fibre a day if you are under 50, and 30 gm a day if you are over 50. Chances are, you are eating far less than that. You can gradually increase your fibre intake over a period of one to two months. Start with half a guava a day. You can get to one guava in a couple of weeks. By then, your large intestine, and the rest of your body, would have adjusted to your new focus on health, and will cooperate. There is also one more thing you must do if you increase your dietary fibre.

Drink more water.

That's right, most of us actually don't drink enough water. A simple rule of thumb is the colour of your urine. Today's best scientific advice is that your urine should range from a light yellow colour to colourless. The yellower your urine, the more dehydrated you are. Feeling thirsty is a sign that you are dehydrated, so listen to your body and drink water when you are thirsty.

Please note that overhydration is not good either. I don't buy into the idea of drinking eight glasses of water a day. This is old advice, and science has moved on. Overhydration can cause electrolyte imbalances and a host of other health problems, and it can be just as big a problem as dehydration, so do not force yourself to drink water when you are showing no signs of thirst. Simply learn to recognize early signs of thirst and deal with them. The important thing is to get the balance right when it comes to drinking water.

I am continually amazed at how many children there are throughout the world who 'don't like the taste of water'. Water has a pure taste, the taste of life itself. If your taste buds have been so corrupted that sugar tastes pure to you and water is tasteless, your odds of maintaining a healthy body and mind are going to be very low.

It is especially important that you make a conscious effort to drink one or two more glasses of water every day when you increase your intake of dietary fibre. This is the surest way of preventing indigestion. So please go ahead, eat half a guava and drink a glass of water now. Cheers!

Why Fibre Is Not Like Cement

Have you ever wondered why cement is the most preferred material for construction in many parts of the world? The main reason is that when you mix it with water, it can be poured, and then when it sets, it stays set and strong for decades. Another reason is that no matter where it is produced, its qualities remain the same, so the strength of anything built with cement can be predicted by architects and engineers. It is this consistency that makes it so prized.

Food-processing companies and manufacturers would like you to think that all fibre is the same, like cement, so they simply add 'fibre' to their products and make you believe that you are looking after your body. Other companies want you to eat supplements of what they call fibre, which again does nothing for the biodiversity in your gut. Eating a fibre supplement is not the same as eating fibre. Justin Sonnenberg of Stanford University makes this point about fibre supplements well in an article by Michael Pollan in the *New York Times* magazine.

Fibre is not a single nutrient...which is why fibre supplements are no magic bullet. There are hundreds of different polysaccharides—complex carbohydrates, including fibre—in plants, and different microbes like to chomp on different ones. To boost fibre, the food industry added lots of a polysaccharide called inulin to hundreds of products, but that's just one kind (often derived from the chicory-plant root) and so may only favor a limited number of microbes. I was hearing instead an argument for a variety of whole grains and a diverse diet of plants and vegetables as well as fruits. The safest way to increase your microbial biodiversity is to eat a variety of polysaccharides…[20]

What other nutrients are we starving our friendly neighbourhood gut bacteria of, by eating the over-processed American diet, which is now being exported all over the world including India? If you want your gut to take care of you, you need to take care of it. Eat more whole foods, more vegetables, fruits, and whole grains. Add fermented foods too. Eat less processed foods with ingredients that may cause damage to the gut lining.

The Benefits of Smoking and a Checklist for Healthy Eating at Parties

This weekend I was at a housewarming party, and the two areas where people congregated were the kitchen/bar and the balcony. I must admit that these days I have become a bit of a bore at parties. One person tells another person that I am a health writer, and people gather around me and insist on having a long discussion on my theories on health. This can be very annoying to other people who couldn't care less, or prefer idle chitchat over deep discussions. Or they have heard what I have to say a dozen times and don't want to hear it again. Next time you are at a party, look at the two groups of people, let's call them the munchers and the smokers. Broadly speaking, no pun intended, you will notice that the munchers are much bigger in girth than the smokers, who look generally lean and fit. There are many reasons why smokers appear this way, of course. It is said that nicotine suppresses hunger. But what if it is not so much about suppressing hunger as about a replacement of munching time? Let us say the average time for smoking a cigarette is six minutes. In this time, the average muncher has gone through about one serving of Doritos, which is about 350 calories including 53 gm of carbohydrates. If a smoker has say five cigarettes during a party, which is on the low side, during this time the muncher has gone through an extra 250 gm of carb junk food. Of course, this is a very simplified model because one can argue that the smoker will finish her cigarette, come into the kitchen and munch to her heart's content. It is also true that even hard-core munchers take breaks from their carb 'inhaling'.

What I am highlighting here is how easy it is to ingest a quarter kilo of junk carbs at a party. Smokers will always consume less than non-smokers because: (1) Nicotine suppresses hunger; (2) time is spent smoking instead of munching; (3) food tastes disgusting after a cigarette; (4) smoking is a distraction from munching.

Do not for a moment think that I support smoking. The simple truth is that smokers live on average fourteen years less than non-smokers. A smoker has a one-in-seven chance of getting lung cancer. This may seem like an acceptable risk to those people who buy lottery tickets along with their cigarettes at the newsagents, and have a one-in-seven million chance of winning the lottery. Smokers are a million times more likely to get lung cancer than win the lottery. Smokers may be lean but they are not fit in any sense of the word. I have yet to find a smoker who is an athlete in any strenuous sport and can compete with a non-smoker of comparable training and talent.

The point I am making is that both munching and smoking at parties have disadvantages. So here is a simple checklist for munchers to have a great time at parties and stay healthy at the same time.

» Do not eat chips, crackers, corn snacks and bread. Instead, serve yourself some of the dip in a bowl, get a small dessert spoon, and just take bites of dip. Eat as much dip as you like; it is a lot healthier than the chips.

» Do not drink beer or white wine. Stick to red wine and whisky. If you must have cocktails, do not have sugary ones. Stay with gin and soda or vodka and soda with a piece of lime.

» Do not save room for dessert. Fill your belly up with extra meat and vegetables.

» Last but not least, do not accept any advice on what to eat from anyone who has more than 20 per cent body fat. Remember that most people have an unconscious drive to remake the world (and their friends) in their own image. That includes me, but then again, I keep my body fat at 12 per cent and my resting heart rate at 55.

I was recently at a gathering where I was answering questions from someone who had a keen interest in health and how to improve his well-being. A dear friend of mine, Pierre, who was sitting opposite me and chain-smoking, was clearly exasperated by our topic of discussion. Probably the last straw for him was when I ordered a large pizza, with extra cheese, double pepperoni and mushrooms, and then proceeded to polish off all the toppings, leaving behind the entire crust. It was not a pretty sight.

Pierre leaned across the table, blew a puff of smoke in my direction and exclaimed in his delicious French accent, 'This is so boring. You always talk about this stuff when we are together. I can tell you that I don't do any of this health stuff, and I am much healthier than you are.'

I am sorry, Pierre, for upsetting you so, and I hereby dedicate the rest of this section to you! But you, dear friend, are nowhere near as healthy as I am. First of all, it is not a competition and you don't get prizes for showing how healthy you are. Each of us is the master of our own body and we make daily choices that affect our health. These choices cumulatively determine not only our lifespan, but also how healthy we are in the last stages of our lives.

If you divide human beings by health outcomes, there are only two broad categories of people: those who smoke, and those who do not. As I have mentioned earlier, smokers live on average fourteen years less than non-smokers. There are many reasons why they die earlier, including heart disease, lung cancer, lung ailments and stroke. Smokers have a metabolic age that is about fourteen years higher than the average, which is why their lifespan is about fourteen years shorter.

Since smokers are leaner than the average person, they

look younger at least for a few years. This lulls them into a false sense of security, and is the ultimate self-deception in human health.

When people ask me for advice on health and wellness, my first question is, 'Do you smoke?' I genuinely have no health advice to offer a smoker other than, 'Quit smoking now.' All your healthy lifestyle habits are eclipsed by the harm caused to your body if you smoke. In other words, if you have decided to be a lifelong smoker, you need not bother with any health tips because they don't apply to you. If you are unable to overcome your smoking habit, which is the 95 per cent cause of your ill-health, then what is the point of worrying about the other 5 per cent? By all means, finish reading this book and then you can put it away until you quit smoking.

Why Spices Are Bad for You

We Indians love spicy food. We also love talking about the health benefits of spices like turmeric, cayenne pepper, garlic, rosemary and cumin. If spices are so good for you, then why are upper-class and middle-class Indians so unhealthy and overweight? Why is diabetes reaching epidemic proportions in India?

The health argument for spices does not really hold in Asia, especially in India, because of the way spices are consumed. The reality is that the two main staples of the Indian diet, rice and wheat, are by themselves bland and tasteless, but when you pair them with a spiced vegetable or lentil or meat curry, you make these health-damaging staples more palatable. Let me repeat, rice, wheat, potatoes and sweets are deadly poisons that are causing the obesity and diabetes epidemic in India today. I am not against whole grains, but against the fact that very few whole grains are consumed in India today. White rice and processed wheat flour or atta are not whole grains, they are just sugar.

Here is a picture of the traditional south Indian thali:

What do we see here? It sure looks appetising! We see a selection of spicy curries arranged in a circle around a heap of rice. To make matters worse, you have yellow rice in one of the bowls on the left, a wheat chapathi on the side, what looks like sweet vermicelli–filled milk next to the chapati, and a bowl of sugar syrup with fried flour dumplings on the right. You are supposed to use the curries as condiments and mix them with the rice. Of course, you are given a second and third helping of rice. There is nothing, I repeat nothing, healthy about the composition of this meal unless you are training for a marathon.

If you wish to live a long and healthy life after the age of thirty, you must slowly reduce, and finally eliminate, rice and wheat from your daily diet. What should you replace them with? The answer is staring back at you from the edge of the thali in the picture. Scale up the size of those small curries and yogurt in the thali, get rid of the dessert, and replace the rice and chapati with stir-fried broccoli, cabbage, cauliflower, carrots. You will have to lessen the spice content in each of the curries if you eat them on their own, without the bland rice.

Here is a picture of a much better thali, from an organic farm in Auroville:

The white rice has been replaced with brown rice, and the rest of the dishes are healthy, wholesome organic fare, full of fibre, nutrtion, and taste. Because the thali is so tasty and unprocessed, you don't need to add too much spice to it.

The best thing of course is to eliminate the rice altogether, at least for one meal a day, and replace it with a cooked vegetable.

Look what happens when you replace rice with broccoli.

Cooked rice

Serving size 1 cup (186.0 gm)

Amount per serving

Calories 242

Calories from fat 4

Total fat 0.4gm

Total carbohydrates 53.2gm

Dietary fibre 0.6gm

Protein 4.4gm

Broccoli

Serving size 1 cup, chopped (88gm)

Amount per serving

Calories 30

Calories from fat 3

Total fat 0.3gm

Total carbohydrates 5.8gm

Dietary fibre 2.3gm

Sugars 1.5gm

Protein 2.5gm

Broccoli has one-eighth the calories of rice. In addition, the carbs in broccoli are slow burning and are not easily absorbed. Even if you eat three–four cups of broccoli you will consume fewer calories than in one cup of rice.

In India, we are lucky to have a breathtaking variety of edible plants. There is no excuse for eating small amounts of healthy plants, while consuming rice and chapatis in vast quantities, like in the thali example given earlier.

What to Feed Your Kids So They Don't Become Fat

Recently I have seen lots of kids, ten to twelve years old, who are overweight. These are urban kids with working parents. Why should kids be overweight in well-to-do families? What must parents be thinking when they allow their children a non-stop supply of sugary drinks, sweets, rice, pasta, bread and wheat products?

According to a widely cited study on childhood obesity:[21]

(Childhood obesity) short-term risks, for orthopedic, neurological, pulmonary, gastroenterological, and endocrine conditions, although largely limited to severely overweight children, are becoming more common as the prevalence of severe overweight rises. The social burden of pediatric obesity, especially during middle childhood and adolescence, may have lasting effects on self-esteem, body image and economic mobility...These studies suggest that risk of cardiovascular disease and all-cause mortality is elevated among those who were overweight during childhood. The high prevalence and dramatic secular trend toward increasing childhood obesity suggest that without aggressive approaches to prevention and treatment, the attendant health and social consequences will be both substantial and long-lasting.

This one is for parents of overweight children

When you, as a parent, look at your obese child, do you even have a clue that the above litany of symptoms is the lifelong gift you are giving your precious child? If you have an overweight child, here is what you should do. Throw out any sugary drinks you have at home. Don't keep any fast carbs at home; that means no pasta, no rice, no wheat, no flour, no bread and no sugar. Get rid of all the loose change at home. Chances are that your child is using the loose change to buy cans of sugary drinks from the corner shop. Of course, there will be howls of protest from your children. Dealing with a sugar-starved child is not easy. Sugar induces cravings and withdrawal symptoms similar to heroin! What should your child eat instead? Fish, meat and eggs; broccoli, cabbage, cauliflower, carrots, peas, peppers, beans.

Here Are Eleven Possible Reasons Why Your Child Is Overweight

» Your child is not getting enough sleep. Lack of sleep is linked to an increased risk of obesity. Fix this problem with strict discipline around sleep times.

» Your child has a television in his bedroom. Seriously? You actually allow this?

» Your idea of dinner at home is pasta, coca cola, French fries and vanilla ice cream.

» Your child's five best friends are all obese. As Jim

Rohn said: 'We are the average of the five people we spend the most time with.'[22]

» You have coins/loose change lying around the house and your child is feeding his or her sugary drink habit with all that spare change.

» Your child is severely stressed. Look for signs your child is being bullied or is otherwise unable to cope with pressure.

» Your child has a medical condition. Pay the paediatrician a visit.

» Your child is having a growth spurt. If the doctor says this is the case, then you have nothing to worry about.

» You think that a fast-food joint is a good alternative to cooking at home.

» Your child is not getting any exercise. If she is not into sports, get her into a running club at least, and use incentives to get her to work out.

» You are giving your child too many antibiotics. The latest research shows a strong link between antibiotic use and obesity.

Fat Is Not Fat, and Salt Is Not Salt...Relax and Enjoy Your Food

The great philosopher Wittgenstein once had a conversation with his friend, Elizabeth Anscombe:

Wittgenstein: Why do people say it is natural to think that the sun goes around the earth rather than that the earth turns on its axis?

Elizabeth: I suppose because it looks as if the sun goes around the earth.

Wittgenstein: Well, what would it look like if the earth turned on its axis?

Elizabeth: ....

What we learn from this exchange is that there are many things in life that we take to be self-evident truths that are in fact pure myths. Some myths are fairly harmless, such as the one that claims if you slather your face with one or the other brand of cream, you will reverse the ageing process. Tens of billions of dollars are spent on this myth, but it doesn't do much damage to public health. Other myths are quite dangerous.

One of the most universal myths that I hear about from virtually everyone I meet concerns dietary fat. Most people believe that eating dietary fat will make you fat, and eating dietary cholesterol will increase your blood cholesterol. This is completely false. First of all, fat is not the culprit, carbohydrates are. Let me explain this using a simple example—a serving of butter will not make you fat, but spreading that butter on bread and eating the bread will. If you are avoiding butter but drinking fruit juices, look at yourself in the mirror. I bet you are wondering why your low-fat, supposedly healthy, juice diet is not working!

Second, a link has never been established between eating dietary cholesterol, such as egg yolks, and an increase in blood cholesterol. Yet even many doctors will tell you to avoid egg yolks. Liquid egg whites are a scam, pure and simple.[23]

My advice on fat in general is this: don't worry about it. Instead avoid sugar and starchy carbs and you will see a dramatic reduction in your percentage of body fat and your risk of developing chronic diseases.

When I went for a routine medical check-up recently,

the doctor asked how much salt I consumed. I was about to answer, but then I inquired, 'Why do you ask?'

He said I should avoid salt to cut the risk of hypertension.

I asked him to name the studies showing a link between salt and hypertension.

He is a doctor and not a researcher, so he had no answer. He did give me a look of mild condescension though, a look that said, 'I am a doctor and I ought to know.'

Intrigued, I went to the Internet to find studies linking salt and hypertension. Guess what, there are none![24]

The truth is that salt is a self-limiting condiment. In other words, in small quantities it greatly enhances the taste of food. In larger quantities, it is revolting and will make you vomit. It is not possible for most of us to consume too much salt because the body has a keen sense of how much is enough, and your taste buds will tell you 'This food is too salty.'

Here is another fact about salt: we humans are essentially walking bags of salt water. Blood, tears, mucus, semen, sweat, urine—these are all salty fluids. The body excretes excess salt, so why should we believe that eating salty foods within reason has any negative effect? The answer, of course, is that it is not salt that is the culprit, but the fact that a lot of junk food tastes good because of the salt. The verdict? Don't worry about salt, instead worry about the chips and the other stuff you are eating with the salt.

What Airline Food Teaches Us about Healthy Eating

How do you maintain healthy eating habits when you are travelling? I get asked this question a lot because I am a frequent traveller. It is true that travelling can be unhealthy, mainly because of the non-availability of healthy foods and the easy availability of convenience foods that are full of sugar and sugary carbs. Airline food, in particular, is designed to pump you full of sugar because sugar and sugary carbs weigh the least when packaged, compared to the calorie punch they deliver, and because they have a long shelf life. I have a simple solution for this problem of airline meals—boiled eggs. I always carry three boiled eggs with me for short-haul flights, and six boiled eggs for long-haul flights. Eggs provide a delicious protein-rich and fatty meal.

This is a picture of your standard United Airlines economy class meal (by Luke Lai):

Note the poisonous bread roll full of fast carbs, the pile of carb noodles, and that seductive sugar-dense slab of dessert.

The bread croissant is 200 calories of poisonous carbs. The noodles are another 200 calories of poison. The sweet dessert, another 400 calories, and a glass of orange juice has 200 calories, including 40 gm of sugar. It adds up to over 1,000 calories if you include the allegedly healthy orange juice!

Now add three boiled eggs to the meal, and you have a delicious protein-filled and fatty meal. What exactly have you done by upgrading your economy class meal with boiled eggs, which have a carb content of zero and a total of 210 calories. When you do the maths, you quickly see that my modified meal is nearly 800 calories less than the previous meal, yet it is as filling, much more nutritious, more delicious and vastly better for your waistline and your health. You get through the flight without spiking your insulin, and arrive at your destination as healthy as ever.

Now here is the best part. You don't have to count calories, starve yourself or even think about any of this. While you are enjoying your dinner, you are actually having a low-calorie meal, and it all happens automatically when you substitute sugary carbs with protein, healthy fats and vegetable carbs. Please do not order juice on the plane. When the drinks trolley comes, people ask for orange juice, thinking it is somehow healthy. Instead, always drink water. And yes, go ahead and have a glass or two of red wine if it helps you sleep! Don't forget that when you follow my diet, you must actually eat a greater quantity of food than you normally do. Yes, you read that right, follow the Baby Elephant Diet and you get to eat more food than normal even as your body fat drops dramatically. As the airline food example above clearly shows, the real pitfalls in everyday eating are the empty carbs you consume. Get rid of these, and you will get rid of your expanding waistline.

Your Real Age Is Not How Long You Have Lived, but How Long You Have Left to Live

I recently met a smoker in his early thirties. He was of average weight, and had around 23 per cent body fat which was well hidden in his calves, hamstrings and around his belly, so it actually looked like he was of average build. What struck me about him was his extremely poor state of health. He had gout, a thyroid problem, his hair was prematurely grey, his skin looked sickly for his age, and he looked almost ten years older than his actual age.

When you are in your thirties, you are at the cusp of your health, when all the bad habits of your twenties are just waiting to come home to roost. When you are in your twenties, you can get away with eating and drinking a lot of junk, sleeping little and exercising even less. But sometime around the age of thirty, your metabolism slows down, your energy levels drop, and taking care of your body becomes essential if you want to enjoy a long and healthy life.

There is scientific consensus that there is something called chronological age, and something else called metabolic age. The former is what we celebrate with candles and cake every year, and the latter is actually how old we really are, biologically speaking. Until the age of thirty, our chronological and metabolic ages roughly keep pace with each other for most of us. But after that, there is a divergence, one way or another, based largely on lifestyle, exercise and diet.

What this means is that if you don't quit smoking, don't give up eating sugary carbs and don't develop a regular exercise and sleep habit by the time you are in your early thirties, you are essentially going to age twice as fast as average, and four times as fast as people who really look after their bodies. It's as simple as that. This is the reason why some fifty-year olds look like they are seventy, while others look like they are thirty!

I have recently started attending my annual high school reunions in India, and I am really struck by the fact that many of my school classmates and even a lot of my juniors could pass for my uncles. These guys have aged rapidly in their thirties and look like they are a couple of decades older than their actual age. Metabolically speaking, their bodies are also much older.

The good news is that metabolic ageing is reversible up to a point. If you make the right changes to your life, starting now, you can take the years off your life, and revert to up to two decades below your chronological age. Yes, it is possible for a fifty-year old to not only look like a thirty-year old but to metabolically function like one too. You just have to look around and see examples of people who look and physically perform like they are twenty years younger than their chronological age. Put another way, someone who lives to be a hundred years old is simply someone whose metabolic age is twenty plus years below their chronological age, which explains how they lived to be a hundred in the first place.

The goal of someone who seeks a healthy lifestyle should be to freeze their metabolic age at thirty, and keep it there for the next twenty years. Beyond fifty, you will, of course, age in all sorts of ways, but if you start with a metabolic age of thirty when you are fifty years old, you are most likely going to live a healthy and active life all the way to hundred.

4

Mind, Body and Diet

Eating Is Not an Alphabetical Roll-Call: Why the Order of Eating Matters

If you follow cricket, you will know why the Indian cricket team's batting order is arranged the way it is. You don't see our best batsmen coming out to bat last. Our batting order is all about putting our best foot forward. The same thing applies to what you eat. The first thing that you put into your mouth when you are hungry is what gets processed first by your body. How do we use this to our advantage?

Let's say you wake up in the morning, and head to the refrigerator. The first thing you reach for is the carton of orange juice or milk. This is the absolute kiss of death as far as your diet in concerned. You see, for those of us who wake up hungry in the mornings—every four out of seven people—that first meal is absolutely important. The other three people couldn't care less if they ate breakfast or not, preferring a small breakfast and large dinner.

But regardless of which category you belong to, the order of eating matters. Don't start your meal with a sugar bomb like a glass of juice or even milk which is liquid calories.

Start it instead with a fruit like guava, papaya, avocado or pomegranate. For lunch or dinner, start your meal with some salad or raw vegetables. This has multiple benefits. First, you are going to eat the healthiest portion of your meal first, so the nutrients are properly absorbed. Second, these items have the fewest calories and the least sugar. Third, they have the highest amount of fibre which creates a nice structure (roughage) for your digestive process to work with. Last but not least, these high-fibre foods fill you up so you eat a bit less of other food items.

'To eat is fine, but to digest is divine,' said someone two hundred years ago. What they meant is that as we get older, our digestive system has to work just that little bit harder to process the food we eat. It is also true that refined and processed food, while unhealthy, is also easy to digest. After all, what can get digested quicker than a spoon of glucose? But the point is that just as we need exercise for the body, all our organs also need a little bit of stress for them to get stronger and stay healthier. 'Use it or lose it' is always the mantra when it comes to the human body, including the digestive system. If you have been feeding it only sugary carbs for thirty years and then suddenly eat a guava, you will likely end up with indigestion. This is not the fault of the guava. Your body is not ready for it. Similarly, if you lead a sedentary life for decades, and then try to run a 5 km race, you will find it difficult.

You will be far better off training your body to eat fibre, and what doctors call 'roughage', every single day. Unlike exercise which takes time and effort, this is actually easy to do. Simply dedicate one shelf in your refrigerator to the Baby Elephant Diet. This shelf should have fibrous fruits and vegetables. Start your day with something from this shelf. The difference in your day will be amazing, even if you don't notice it at first. Your morning toilet routine will become more regular and easy, with the fibre and roughage making for easy passage. Illnesses like piles, acid reflux, gas and indigestion will disappear. Your mood will improve palpably. You won't suffer hunger pangs, your stomach will feel comfortably full all the time and your energy levels will stay constant throughout the day. You won't get as many food cravings, so you are less likely to turn to comfort food.

The thing about good health is that when we have it, we don't spend a moment thinking about it, and when we don't have it, we think of nothing else. For the sake of your health, I want you to develop habits that take very little effort; habits that will be to your body what a regular tune-up is to your car. As every mechanic will tell you, it is far better to take preventive steps for your car, so that you 'solve' problems before they develop. This is true of your body as well.

Speaking of cars and mechanics, oil is not only good for lubricating your automobile, it is also essential for your body. I am not talking about engine oil here of course, but about the oils that are part of the human diet, such as olive oil, nut oils and vegetable oils.

Oils in the Diet

There are many cleansing rituals in ayurveda that involve the use of oils, both orally as well as in enemas. Oil is nothing but 100 per cent fat. Over the past few decades, we have been conditioned by Western medicine, and largely American-led conventional wisdom, to believe that fat is bad for us. Well, guess what? The latest research shows that this view is totally false. As any ayurvedic doctor will tell you, fat is good for you. In fact, Western science has done such a U-turn that several recent studies show that people who eat lots of nuts have the best health outcomes. The biggest component of nuts is nut oil, which is released when you chew nuts and swallow them.

I want you to pay careful attention to the oil/fat in your diet because, along with fibre and protein, it represents the third pillar of good health. It is essential for good health. Oil and fat are the same, and unfortunately fat has had a bad reputation for decades, thanks to a totally false notion of what causes heart disease (the real culprit is sugar, not fat).

The Baby Elephant Diet is largely about eating fibre and avoiding fast carbs, but one cannot discuss nutrition without talking about essentials fats and oils. In this section we will talk about what makes a good oil, and at the end of the section, narrow down on the best oil for lasting health—the answer may surprise many of you.

I have discussed elsewhere in this book that eating fats is not only good for you, it is essential for weight loss. It is crucial that you stop using sugar as your primary source of calories, and get more of your sustenance from fat. Protein is also important, but mainly for people who want to build and maintain lean muscle mass. Even if you are not interested in a shapely muscular body, the advice is the same; switch from carbohydrates to fats.

But which fats should you eat?

There is an enormous amount of misinformation regarding oils, so it is important to get your facts straight. The types of oils we eat fall under the following categories: monounsaturated fatty acids (MUFAs), e.g. olive oil; polyunsaturated fatty acids (PUFAs), e.g. rapeseed or corn or groundnut oil; hydrogenated trans fats, e.g. dalda, margarine; animal fats, e.g. beef fat which is less common in India; and milk fats, e.g. ghee, butter, yogurt, milk.

First I am going to tell you what not to eat. Do not consume hydrogenated or partially hydrogenated fats, like palmoline, dalda or margarine, which are poisonous for your heart. These fats are also found in almost all packaged foods and snacks. Act as if the total amount of hydrogenated fats you can eat in a lifetime is fixed and you have to spread this amount over your entire life. If you want to stay healthy and live to ninety, cut down your consumption of this poison.

You should replace hydrogenated fats with good, old-fashioned butter or ghee. Yes, butter and ghee, especially freshly made, are excellent for health if consumed in moderation. Butter and ghee will actually help you lower your body fat, keep your body and skin healthy and vastly improve the flavour of your food. Don't worry too much about what a moderate amount is. If you are eating fewer grains like rice and wheat, then the butter and ghee you consume will automatically be moderated.

Eat egg yellows, which are full of healthy fat. They are excellent for health and many of us also find them delicious. One comment about eggs though. Today, factory farming has reared its ugly head in India like in the US and the eggs available are cheap and not as healthy as free-range eggs. In my opinion, an egg should cost Rs 6-8 instead of its existing retail price of Rs 4 and should be free range. At my farm in

Hyderabad, chickens are given plenty of land to roam and they munch on worms and other tidbits they find in the soil. We give them some seeds and grains to supplement their diet. If you as consumers demand healthier eggs, and are willing to pay more for them, the market will respond. This has already happened in rich countries where there are all sorts of egg varieties to choose from.

Now let's talk about oils or unsaturated fats, which we use in our daily cooking and in salads. There are broadly two types of unsaturated fats: omega-3 and omega-6. Most oils have both kinds of fat. What matters is the proportion of these two. A 1:1 proportion between these two fats is ideal.

Unfortunately, most cooking oils have very little omega-3 and far too much of omega-6. This is especially true of so-called healthy cooking oils like sunflower, rapeseed (canola) or safflower. The problem with these oils is twofold: firstly, too much omega-6 is bad for you and secondly, when you cook at high heat with these oils, they become partially hydrogenated and turn into poisonous trans fats. Healthy oils like olive and flaxseed are good for you but only if you consume them in salad dressings and don't heat them.

When you are cooking or frying, saturated fat is really your best friend, because it has a shelf life, it does not spoil, and it is stable at high temperatures. Ghee is excellent for cooking. Isn't that surprising? If you want to use a vegetable oil for cooking and frying, it turns out that the healthiest is actually coconut oil which is cheap, plentiful and easy to extract. Our relationship with coconuts goes back to the beginnings of primate history. We have literally evolved to eat coconuts.

Gut Microbes

Here is an astonishing new scientific discovery, probably the most important in this century regarding human health. Microbes in your gut dictate your moods, your drive and hugely influence your brain.

I have long been a fan of good bacteria, and in fact my first book, *All about Bacteria*, looked extensively into the positive role of bacteria for health. But in the two years since that book was published, our understanding of bacteria has improved, so it is time to talk about gut bacteria and their role once again.

Science has known for some time that the human body has around 100 trillion cells, of which an astonishing 90 per cent are bacteria that live on us and inside us in a massive ecosystem that resembles a village pond or a coral reef. Of these 90 trillion bacterial cells, 90 per cent live in our gut, which is really the engine room of the human ship. Thousands of species live there, a teeming and vibrant and diverse microbiota. The health of the ship relates directly to the health of this engine room.

While these members of the human ecosystem influence our behaviour in myriad ways, it is ultimately our mind which controls them. Think about it. If they had the capacity to imagine, they would think of our brain as some kind of god or nature spirit that feeds them at regular intervals and makes the human ship they inhabit move from place to place. So clearly, while they have a lot of influence, we are still very much in charge to the extent that we possess, and use, our free will. Our dietary choices in turn influence what kind of an ecosystem develops inside our gut. It is already well known that the gut of healthy people is very different from that of unfit or unhealthy people.

Now I want to show you how to make friends with your gut microbe friends.

I want you to pause and do this simple experiment even as you are reading this book. Close your eyes for a moment, and visualize in your mind's eye the Great Barrier Reef off the Australian coast. Close your right nostril with your right thumb, and take a slow deep breath through your left nostril. Now with your right little finger, close the left nostril, open your right nostril by releasing the thumb, and exhale, slowly and deeply. Next, inhale slow and deep with the right nostril. Finally close your right nostril with your thumb, open your left nostril by releasing the little finger, and exhale. Repeat this pattern for about six to seven minutes.

Next visualize part of the Great Barrier Reef living inside your gut, enveloped by YOU. Its nourishing, life-giving qualities are seeping through your body every moment of your existence. Feel the positive energy it emits as it pulses through your system. Feel your spine tingle and shivers forming in waves coursing up your spine. Feel the warmth as your body heats up. Now slowly open your eyes.

How can you not be an environmentalist after you feel this? Can you see now that there is no difference between looking after your own body and looking after nature? People who treat nature as a giant disposable vending machine that can be consumed and dumped in a landfill are unlikely to look at their bodies any differently. There is, of course, a small percentage of people who lack empathy for others and for their environment. We call them sociopaths.

But coming back to the gut, it turns out that the old adage 'you are what you eat' is absolutely correct. The gut microbes of fit people are different from those of obese people. The moods of fit people are different from the moods of the unfit.

From here, it is not a great leap to come up with diets that actually improve your mood. Unfortunately, this whole space has been taken over by the manufactured food industry, which discovered a long time ago that sugar is more addictive than cocaine. The result is a whole host of cheap sugar drinks and savoury snacks (savoury snacks are still processed sugar) which appear to make you feel good, while in fact all they are doing is giving you a drug-like high while saddling you with horrific chronic illnesses.

So let us take back our health and our gut from these food companies. In reality, what makes you content and positive is healthy, wholesome, organically grown food. It is disingenuous in the extreme to argue that the composition of an organic tomato is the same as that of a conventional tomato. That would perhaps be true if you looked at the chemical composition of the tomato, but what about its biological composition? An organic tomato has higher-quality dominant genes, because it is a hardier specimen than a conventional tomato. An organic tomato has been exposed to a more biodiverse environment, making it more adaptable and more genetically diverse.

The Purpose of the Large Intestine

This book is all about fibre, and one cannot discuss fibre without a close look at the body's 'coral reef', namely the large intestine. We have previously discussed that there are essentially four chambers in the digestion process. The mouth and oesophagus are where the food we eat gets an enzyme bath. The stomach is where the food gets an acid bath and where any pathogens are destroyed. The mix of enzyme, food and acid is called chyme, which then enters the small intestine. In the small intestine, pancreatic juices are added, along with bicarbonate that lessens the acidity of the chyme. Most of the sugars and protein from food are absorbed into the body from the small intestine.

Chyme spends around two to six hours in the small intestine, and then passes into the fourth chamber, the large intestine, along with most of the fibre. It spends six to seventy-two hours in the large intestine, where the fibre is fermented by gut bacteria. There are at least a thousand species of bacteria, and probably over 80 trillion bacterial cells! Yes, your large intestine is a 5-foot-long pond ecosystem. Food enters it as a liquid, and leaves it as a solid, so one of the key roles of the large intestine is to remove water from the food.

Many of the nutrients from fibre are broken down and turned into essential nutrients by bacteria here. We know that vitamin K and vitamin B are produced by bacteria in the large intestine. In addition, several key antibodies are produced here. The large intestine is literally our own private bio-reactor. Although we understand only a small amount of how this process really works, there is no question that having a healthy bio-reactor is the key to good health.

There is a direct link between lack of fibre in the diet and a whole host of illnesses including obesity, diabetes,[25] heart disease[26] and high blood pressure.[27] It should be quite obvious why this is the case. If you are eating energy-dense foods and sugars, most of the excess calories are going to get absorbed in the small intestine. If your large intestine has less fibre to ferment, you are going to feel less full, and are more likely to overeat the same junk food that gets processed in the small intestine. You will also end up with nutrient deficiencies because you are not getting the benefit of the fermentation process that happens in the large intestine.

Next time you drink that glass of 'real' orange juice, imagine what happens to it in your body. Virtually none of it will make it to your large intestine. All the sugar in the juice will get absorbed inside the small intestine, raising your blood sugar, causing a big insulin spike, which in turn will convert the sugar into belly fat. If this process is repeated often, your body can develop resistance to insulin, which leads to diabetes. You think you are drinking something healthy, but in fact you are doing exactly the opposite.

Processed food is bad for you in many ways, but the most basic reason it is so detrimental to your health is that it has little or no fibre. Even when the processed food does have fibre, like many breakfast cereals, the amount of sugar that's added to it makes it very unhealthy to eat.

So, if you want to make a change in your diet and lifestyle, just focus on keeping your large intestine healthy by feeding it fibre every day. You will see a huge difference in your state of health and wellness. Your energy levels will be more stable throughout the day, you will be less susceptible to colds and illnesses, and both your physical and mental well-being will improve. Let us look at practical and simple ways of harnessing this power of the large intestine.

The Vaastu Shastra of Human Relations

Do you know that the vast majority of Indians believe in vaastu shastra, the ancient science of architecture and construction? I bet you are one of those people. Even if you are not an active believer, I will wager that you have been exposed to vaastu shastra in your life, maybe even in the design of your home. Even if you want to buy a non-vaastu home, it is likely that no builder will build you one. And even if you are successful in building it, you will probably have trouble selling it in the future.

So is there a vaastu equivalent for human relations? Apparently there is, and there is scientific evidence that supports human vaastu. Remember the Jim Rohn quote I spoke of in the context of Aunty Sunita's friends? 'You are the average of the five people that you spend the most time with.'

This has got to be one of the most profound statements in human psychology. Essentially, what Jim Rohn is saying is that a large part of how successful you become in life depends on the people you spend time with. There are always exceptions to any rule in psychology, but I bet this rule applies to the vast majority of us. You can think of this as the vaastu of human relations. Fundamentally, this goes back to human evolution as social animals. We are hard-wired to be empathetic to other humans. The simple observation that yawning is contagious is true, as many scientific studies have shown.[28] We are constantly influenced by the feelings, actions and words of the people around us. I apply this rule in my daily life all the time. I try to spend most of my time with people who inspire me, and, above all, I try to make sure that my young children are part of a studious, creative group of friends and not of any group that is likely to lead them down the wrong path.

Now what does the vaastu of human relations have to do with your diet, fitness and wellness? Quite a lot, it seems. Researchers have found that your choice of dinner companion influences what you eat.[29] When you are selecting a meal in a restaurant or a cafeteria, if someone in your group chooses an unhealthy high-carbohydrate meal, then you are also much more likely to indulge in the same meal. Similarly, if other people in the group choose a salad or other healthy options, then you are likely to follow suit. This is quite a significant finding, and one that is backed by a lot of anecdotal evidence. Next time you go to a restaurant, see how people in groups order. It will not surprise you that unhealthy eaters generally stick together and so do people who care about healthy eating. You can witness this behaviour at a school or a college. Notice how the fit and attractive people stick together in one group, while the unfit and unhealthy ones are in another group. While these choices may seem unconscious, the reality is that we can make conscious choices simply by being aware of this human tendency.

When I was in college, initially I spent more time with students who partied a lot. My grades suffered because of this. Then I took a running class and started hanging out with runners who were fit and focused. To my surprise, I became fitter and more focused, and my grades improved.

We can all use this power of company to our advantage. Today, with online groups that can be found on websites like www.meetup.com, we can all find new groups to meet and interact with. If you find a running group or a zumba class or a climbing group to join, it will make a tremendous difference to your fitness levels and to your diet.

In India, I frequently come across social groups of upstanding citizens, such as Rotary and Roundtable, where members spend time on scotch appreciation, socializing and the like. These groups, I am sorry to say, have not yet adopted healthy-eating lifestyles, and my fond hope is that they can be convinced to do so.

This book is all about nutrition, but let us not forget that it is also a self-help book. I am here to educate you on what to eat and how to eat for good health, but I am more than an author. I am also an activist. I want to motivate you to make positive changes in all areas of your life, and the first step is to give you a workable plan on how to improve your nutritional health. I have spent lots of time studying the lives of successful people, self-made people who have built businesses and done amazing things. I have looked for common factors such as intelligence, hard work, education levels, family background and fitness levels among these people. What I found was that none of these factors matters for success, well-being and wellness. The only common factor I found was that these people all kept the right company. Invariably, the people they spent time with were also highly motivated, committed, successful individuals.

This is especially true if your goal is fitness, wellness and nutrition. There is one easy thing you can do before you start a fitness programme or start to follow my diet. Find a group of people who are also doing it, and who appreciate you and motivate you. Believe me, the people around you have helped you get where you are in the first place. If you attempt to change your diet and become a new person, they will undermine your efforts. Not because they don't love you, but because your new initiative will make them uncomfortable, and you will no longer fit into their image of you if you succeed. In a country like India, social bonds are strong, and social pressures are far stronger than in Western countries where individuals have more freedom to act and there are fewer social conventions. I have numerous friends who started following my diet, only to be undermined by their wives who suddenly developed an interest in making fresh samosas or buying unhealthy snacks.

Get a Guru Even for a Little While

Most of us do not have the luxury of thinking about every aspect of our daily lives. As a professional writer, I actually earn my living examining life, habits and best practices, and experimenting various techniques on myself. I see myself as your personal curator, someone who researches and finds the best in preventive health techniques. That does not really make me a guru, however. A guru is someone you ideally develop a personal relationship with. There are people out there who dedicate their lives to spiritual practices and holistic and preventive health techniques. These are the real gurus, and I highly recommend that everyone have a guru for at least part of their spiritual journey. Of course, I realize that most of us are busy, and taking time out for a spiritual journey, let alone going on a quest for a guru, is a luxury. But I am hoping to plant a seed here, in these pages. When you are ready, you will automatically make time for it. It is sometimes said that when you are ready, the guru finds you, but perhaps this is a self-fulfilling prophecy.

The reason why a spiritual retreat or a course can be a transformational experience is often because it shakes you out of your existing patterns. One form of meditation called vipassana makes you live in complete silence for ten days, alone with your thoughts and a guided meditation programme. Other gurus teach you to breathe differently, and will initiate you into kriya yoga, an extraordinarily powerful practice that can fundamentally alter your mind, your personality and your health. The study of human consciousness and the melding of mind and body has been the realm of Hinduism for thousands of years. Today, there are Western clones trying to imitate some of these practices, but remember that these cannot work out of context. Indeed, you can cause great damage to yourself if you attempt these techniques without the help of a guru.

Luckily, there are plenty of gurus in India who can cater to people of all faiths. You don't have to lose your faith, or even gain it if you don't have any, in order to access spirituality, which is India's true contribution to the world. Just as one can attend a Christian convent for secondary school and not become a Christian, you can access Hindu spiritual practices while keeping your own faith and traditions.

Why Does Kriya Work?

Westerners are trying to strip away the faith elements behind powerful Hindu and Buddhist spiritual practices, and turn kriya into something they call 'mindfulness' in order to make it secular. While I disagree with taking spiritual practice out of its context, a detailed discussion of this aspect will be a digession from the purpose of this book. Let us, instead, discuss why kriya and its spiritually impoverished cousin 'mindfulness' both have an impact on your physical health.

At a scientific level, Western neuroscientists have discovered that kriya fundamentally alters the functioning of the brain, making us less reactive to stress.[30] The research is new and ongoing, but given that physical symptoms like obesity, heart disease and diabetes are all stress related, it is obvious that anything that helps us cope better with stress will have a dramatic positive impact on health.

But kriya goes much further than that. Ultimately, all functions in the body are reducible to electrical impulses. Human senses and actions such as eating, breathing, exercise and thinking, are forms of implementation. All these either cause, or are caused by, electrical impulses in the brain. Kriya is so powerful, it can directly manipulate these impulses, and quickly alter your existing patterns and habits. A simple example is the use of kriya as an anaesthetic during surgery. Just as a painkiller releases endorphins and calms the brain, kriya can do the same thing without any drugs. A simple form of kriya, known in the West as hypnosis, has been used as an anaesthetic and there are well-documented studies that it works. Kriya is powerful, but it cannot be learned from reading a book. You have to practise it regularly.

In its complexity, kriya yoga is like advanced mathematics. It is completely incomprehensible to those who have not learned it, in the same way that a bunch of equations on a whiteboard are incomprehensible to those who have not studied maths. Just as simpler forms of maths are used by us every day, simple kriya techniques are behind many of our daily human interactions, as well as our subconscious and unconscious actions. By learning and practising kriya, you automatically learn to recognize patterns of behaviour in yourself as well as others. This leads to tremendous positive changes in your personality, reduction in stress levels and a much sounder body and mind.

This brings us back to the Baby Elephant Diet. The reason understanding nutrition is so important is that it is an action (eating) that we perform several times a day, every day.

Unlike spiritual practice or exercise, both of which are voluntary actions, eating and sleeping are two easy actions that we have to perform each day because our body requires us to. It is very clear that in the modern world, we get far too much of the former and far too little of the latter.

The Way Children Eat a Dosa Can Predict Their Success in Life

Sanaa was nervous. Kabir, her boyfriend of two years, had come home to meet her parents for the first time. Everyone knew this was the big moment. Would they approve of him, or would she have to break it off? It was unthinkable to go against the wishes of her parents, and her grandmother, the wise matriarch of the house. How are they going to react to Kabir? The two of them were so much in love, and everything was so beautiful between them. The first half hour had gone off okay, but her grandmother seemed a bit cool, a bit distant. There were some pointed questions from her father about family background, career, ambition. Everyone was looking for a sign from her grandmother, any sign, but her face was nearly expressionless.

At last, it was time for lunch. A sumptuous sit-down meal, and everyone was sitting around the table. And what's this? The first course was a dosa. Sanaa frowned. She could not remember ever eating a dosa at lunchtime, let alone as an opening course of a big lunch with so many dishes… What was going on? Kabir did not know this, of course, and he took it in his stride, chatting with everyone with nervous laughter and trying not to feel self-conscious. As Sanaa looked across at Kabir, she saw him put condiments on the side of his plate. He then carefully ate the dosa, eating the softer middle first, then leaving a perfect ring of the crispy outer edge of the dosa, and then finally savouring the crispy edge on its own, dipped lightly in chutney. Watching this, her grandmother's eyes softened, and she broke into a wide grin, and the whole family visibly relaxed. Sanaa felt elation swelling up inside her; everything was going to be fine!

What just happened? Can the way a person eats a dosa predict anything about their personality? Scientists have shown that it actually can. Well, they haven't actually tested people using a dosa, but there was a famous test done in the late 1960s at Stanford University called the 'Marshmallow test'.[31] Walter Mischel came up with research on delayed gratification that scientists today call the 'Marshmallow test'. In this test, a researcher gave participants a marshmallow (a corn and gelatin sweet that's common in the US) and said to them, 'If you can wait five minutes until I come back before you eat it, you can have two marshmallows when I return.' Apparently 30 per cent of the children were able to wait patiently, while the other 70 per cent could not. Amazingly, the 30 per cent who waited went on to do much better in life, academically, career-wise and in relationships, than the rest of the children.

So how does this translate into dosas? Very simple. What Sanaa's wise old grandmother picked up on was this. The way Kabir ate his dosa showed a patient man who believed in delayed gratification. This was the kind of young man who would save for a comfortable retirement and think about the long-term security of his family. In short, the perfect son-in-law!

Before you rush off to do the dosa test on someone you know, think about your own situation. How do you eat? How do you delay your gratification? If you want dessert, do you wait for the appropriate mealtime or occasion, or do you need to have it immediately? Be honest with yourself when you answer these questions.

The good news is that delayed gratification is a learned trait. By teaching yourself to wait, just a while, for that treat, you are not only taking control of your body and your mind, but you are actually putting into motion a whole set of related behaviours that will have a positive impact on your life. When that new phone model or new season clothes or shoes are launched, do you have to rush out to buy them? Do you have to see that movie on the first day of its release? Compulsive behaviour is linked to poor life and relationship outcomes, and you can start to change this tendency by taking charge of what you put into your mouth, and when you put it. If you have a problem with compulsiveness, chant this mantra—'*Delay gratification*'—each morning when you wake up. In fact, make a big sign and hang it in your room so it is the first thing you see when you wake up. Slow down your reaction time to everyday annoyances. In the same way that a slow digestion is a healthy digestion, slow reaction means a lower level of stress and a higher threshold of tolerance. These are the secrets to long life and great health.

It turns out that the best strategy to delay gratification

is actually distraction. In other words, don't even think about that rasmalai in the refrigerator. Instead, occupy your mind by listening to music, reading a book, talking to a friend, etc. The most important thing though is to develop delay strategies. Food is usually the first area where children, for whom hunger is such a powerful emotion, learn about delay tactics. The relationship we develop with food also tends to stay with us for a long long time, so it is important to develop good habits early. But it is never too late to reprogramme ourselves.

The single most important skill for success in virtually any sphere is self-control, but we don't always teach this to our children. Self-control is an independent skill that once acquired, translates into every part of our lives, not just food.

Now here is the amazing part. Our personalities are not hard-coded. In other words, we largely develop patterns of how we behave, based on our circumstances. For instance, if you grew up in Kerala and you are a man, you would wear a mundu and grow a moustache because that is what every man around you does. But the same man growing up in Delhi would wear a shirt and pant, and the moustache would be optional.

At any point in life, we can reprogramme ourselves, and the way we can do it is to learn the science and art of self-control in whatever field we are comfortable with. For example, let's say you have a tendency to overeat. It would be extremely difficult for you to learn to control your diet immediately. But let's say you also love learning languages, and it comes naturally to you. If you set yourself a goal of learning a new language through a structured programme, and then accomplish that goal (even though you did so because you loved doing it), then the self-control that you learned during that process will later translate into self-control in dealing with food. Just as you can't learn a new language immediately or pick up a violin and play it without practising, you can't just stop eating if you don't first learn self-control in an area where you can follow through. So start developing self-control as an independent skill, but in areas of your life where you have the most talent and interest. If you love music, organize your library. If you are at your best in the morning, make an extra effort to go to bed early so you wake up and enjoy the morning.

In the context of diet, delayed gratification means eat the fibre first (and in the largest quantity), protein next, fat third and carbohydrate/sugar last (and in the smallest quantity). It also means waiting for the cheat day before tucking into that piece of chocolate cake. People who delay gratification are also naturally able to respond to stress better, according to the Marshmallow test. It seems that the ability to refrain from reacting in the presence of a delectable treat will also prevent us from reacting aggressively in the presence of stress.

This is such important advice, that I will reiterate it later in the book.

How Stress, Obesity and Diabetes Are Linked

Here is an amazing truth, but something which most people do not know. If you are obese and have type 2 diabetes, losing any excess weight will put your diabetes into remission. It really is as simple as that, but, of course, it is easier said than done, as many people who struggle daily with obesity can tell you.

Now here is an interesting fact. When your body is stressed, it releases stress compounds, namely adrenaline and cortisol.

These hormones are there to give us a short-term energy boost, and they are part of the 'fight or flight' response. In the case of sudden, acute stress, your body is pumped with adrenaline. Adrenaline raises the heart rate, increases blood pressure, expands the air passages in your lungs, distributes blood to the muscles and makes your cells resistant to insulin (a hormone that lowers blood glucose), in order to maximize the blood glucose available for your muscles and your brain. This temporary insulin resistance when you are under stress, can be looked at in another way, as a temporary form of diabetes, because diabetes happens either when your body produces too little insulin, or your cells become resistant to insulin.

What if your stress is not acute (as happens when, say, you are chased by an angry dog), and it is more chronic (you have an abusive boss, an irritating spouse or you are worried about your mortgage). The stress hormone that gets produced is not adrenaline, but another one called cortisol. Cortisol works in a similar fashion to adrenaline, but it is a chronic stress hormone. Chronic stress causes insulin resistance, which is nothing but diabetes. It also causes sustained high blood pressure, and prompts the body to produce cholesterol, which in some people turns into plaque in the arteries. Plaque is the main culprit in heart disease.

The other insidious side effect of stress and the high cortisol that comes with it is obesity. Human studies[32] have demonstrated that cortisol injections increase appetite and cause sugar cravings, resulting in obesity. The same studies show that premenopausal women who secreted/produced more cortisol ate foods high in sugar and fat. It seems that cortisol influences food consumption by binding to receptors in the brain and induces people to eat food that is high in sugar, which causes obesity. Remember that advertisement for a large so-called 'milk chocolate' manufacturer that asks you to eat their product whenever you feel sad? Never mind that milk chocolate is a sugar candy and is not actually chocolate. Basically this company wants to hook you to its products by asking you to eat sugar when you are feeling low. This sugar, of course, causes another low once its effects wear off. Don't fall for these marketing gimmicks.

It turns out that excess fat cells that are stored in the body are themselves what scientists call 'free radicals'. These free radicals are very damaging in that they cause the body to be permanently stressed, which increases the production of cortisol. Once you get into the vicious cycle of obesity and stress, the downward spiral gets out of control. Stress causes obesity, and obesity causes stress. The good news is that what is a vicious cycle can be turned into a virtuous one too. If your weight goes down, your stress goes down too, and vice versa.

But we must always remember that the underlying reasons for obesity and chronic stress are the same—it all begins with the mind. If you don't address the underlying issues, you are much less likely to succeed in your health goals.

Stress and Irritable Bowel Syndrome, Ulcerative Colitis and Other Immune Illnesses

Scientists have recently concluded that the vast majority of immune illnesses that affect the gut are actually stress related.[33] For those of us who grew up thinking that disease is caused by pathogens, genes, or simply old age, it should be a wake-up call to learn that most illnesses are actually caused by stress.

It really is all in your mind!

But it is too simplistic to look at stress and hormones on their own. The 80 trillion bacterial cells that live in your gut play a part too. The health of these bacteria has a direct impact on the health of your body, and it is here that science has made rapid strides in these past few years. It is now accepted in science that your gut bacteria can influence your moods, your stress levels and your behaviour.[34]

There are, of course, several ways of dealing with stress, but my focus in this book is on the nutritional approach. Since so much of your health and bodily functions are determined by what you eat, the simplest approach to dealing with stress is to eat stress-reducing foods.

The number one culprit in increasing stress in your gut is lack of fibre in the food you eat. Of course, there is an optimum range of fibre, and too much is not good either.

You Are Not Alone

I have worked with some of the most successful and wealthy people in India and around the world. I have even worked with people who run large healthcare companies and hospitals. No one would look at them and say there was any deficit in their lives. But there is always an underlying factor for their obesity and diabetes. Sometimes it is simply a lack of awareness about themselves, or a lack of focus on their bodies. But often, there is a major source of stress in their lives. When I work with individuals, I try to understand what that source of stress is. When I find it, I usually can't change it, but nine out of ten times I can change the person's response to it.

And that is the crux of the matter. There is always stress

in life, no one is immune to it, but how you respond to the stress is important. A common response to stress is to develop an unhealthy relationship with food. The reason unhealthy food is called 'comfort food' is because it really does take your mind off stress. Unfortunately, it solves nothing and, instead, creates a health problem to add to your stress.

What you need are simple tools that can change your response to stress, that can break your unhealthy eating patterns and force a positive change in your life. This section, focused on the mind, will provide you with those tools. I can talk about what to eat and when to eat all day long, but only your mind controls and ultimately rationalizes what goes into your mouth.

Most people who are obese blame their genes. They are also in total denial about how many calories they eat daily and the unhealthy food they are eating. I know people who are frustrated because they walk 5 km a day and yet are obese. When I point out that a regular 5-km walk will burn about 150 calories, which is what is found in one can of cola, they look confused. They can't understand this maths. In other words, cut out the cola and the fruit juices, and each glass you don't drink is worth a 5-km walk. But you see, walking *feels* like you are making more of an effort than simply not drinking cola. So your brain thinks that the effect of walking must be more. But it is not.

Sleep, the Single Most Important Determinant of Your Health

In a book about nutrition, it may or may not surprise you to find a section on sleep, but it is so important that no book on nutrition and dieting is complete without addressing sleep. Why do living things sleep? I say living things because not only do animals sleep, plants sleep too. So do microbes, including bacteria. Have you ever wondered how migrating birds sleep when they are flying over long distances? They actually divide their brains into two halves, and one half can sleep while the other half continues to help the birds fly and navigate. This is called unihemispheric slow wave sleep, and it is practised by birds as well as some animals. I am only citing this example because it shows the ingenuity of evolution to accommodate the need of all creatures for physical and mental rest at regular intervals.

Therefore, 'downtime' is built into life itself. The most plausible explanation is that sleep allows repair of cell damage, where the normal activities of cells are put on the slow burner or shut down, while repairs take place. In humans, with our capacity for reason and abstract thought, sleep also has the additional task of converting short-term memories into long-term ones, and in restoring the tired mind.

Sleep has a huge role to play in nutrition, wellness and health. There is overwhelming evidence that obesity is linked to too little sleep.[35] How much sleep we need varies from person to person, but the human range seems to be four to ten hours a day, with the vast majority of us needing between six and eight hours. The easiest way for most of us to understand how much sleep we need is to go to bed without an alarm for a few nights. You will soon see that you wake up naturally after six to eight hours, which is your daily requirement.

Have you ever blamed your genes for your health? People who do this are not wrong. But they are not entirely right either. What scientists have discovered recently on this subject provides an amazing insight into how much of a role genes play in poor health. It turns out that the effect of genes on obesity, mental illness, diabetes, heart disease, etc., depends on the amount of sleep you get. In other words, if you are sleeping less than seven hours a night, your genetic traits that control obesity, are more likely to express themselves.[36] What this means is that if your genetic makeup consists of obesity (if your parents/grandparents were obese), you cannot hope to maintain a healthy weight through diet and exercise alone, unless you are getting enough sleep.

I would go so far as to say that the first thing you must do to get fit and stay fit is to sleep as much as your body requires. I am always amazed at the number of people I see in the gym who are sleep-deprived and unfit. They would be much better off, from a health standpoint, spending their free time sleeping instead of working out in the gym. In fact, one of the worst things you can do if you are sleep-deprived is strength training or any other strenuous workout. If you do not allow your body to sleep and repair the cell damage caused by exercise, you are going to do a lot of damage to your body.

The link between lack of sleep and obesity does not stop here. British scientists have found an intriguing link between the amount of light in your bedroom when you are sleeping and obesity.[37] Scientists still do not know exactly why this is the case, but one possible culprit is the hormone melatonin, which is a sleep regulator in humans. Your sleep quality gets affected without adequate amounts of melatonin. Since melatonin is produced in darkness, you should definitely take steps to reduce the amount of light in your bedroom.

5
What to Eat

The Specifics of the Baby Elephant Diet: What to Eat Each Day

Breakfast

Breakfast is the most important meal of the day for four out of seven people. But whether it is a big meal for you or a small one, the most important thing is that breakfast sets the tone for the entire day, so it is important to get it right. Another good thing about breakfast is that most of the time you are going to eat it at home, so it is more a question of educating your family on what are the right foods to prepare in the morning.

The good news is that there is less peer pressure in the morning, so there really is no reason for you to eat junk for breakfast. The bad news is that you almost certainly eat junk during the day, so you need to modify your food habits at breakfast.

Here are the worst things to eat for breakfast:

1. Orange juice or juice of any kind
2. Bananas, mangoes, watermelon, grapes
3. Idli is deadly

4. Rice or rice derivatives
5. Chapathis
6. Toast
7. Cereals
8. Skim milk
9. Oats

Now you are looking at this list and thinking, 'Do I really want to follow this guy's diet? He is banning pretty much everything I eat in the morning.' But just look at this list. The only food items that have fibre are bananas, mangoes and cereals. But these are also full of sugar and carbohydrates and will give you a massive sugar high in the morning, leading to all sorts of problems later in life. Oats also fall in this category. Many nutrition experts recommend oats, but I am sorry to say that I do not agree. Oats raise your blood sugar really quickly. That can't be good. Although they do contain fibre, my research shows that the sugar absorption is way too much for the fibre to compensate.

So what can you eat?

Here are the best things you can eat for breakfast:

1. Eggs (both white and yellow)
2. Guava
3. Papaya
4. Avocado
5. Dal dosa
6. Chia seeds in full-fat milk
7. Spinach, amaranth or any leafy vegetable, stir-fried or in a soup
8. Full-fat yogurt

9. Nuts like almonds and walnuts
10. One slice of whole-grain toast with any of the other nine items

Yes. You can eat really well for breakfast but it is important to avoid a big sugar bomb first thing in the morning. Give your body and your large intestine a healthy dose of fibre at breakfast, and the rest of your day will go smoothly, with a steady dose of energy available for all your activities.

Lunch

I have previously talked about why six small meals a day is a bogus concept. It only works for about 10 per cent of the population. So I am going to assume that most of us eat one or two big meals and one or two smaller meals or snacks a day.

For lunch, a bowl of dal, with a few sprinkles of rice on top is a good meal if you are in a hurry, followed by a bowl of full-fat curd with again a few sprinkles of rice if you must. If you want to be slightly more elaborate, add a side of vegetables, say okra or beans or tinda which can be consumed in unlimited quantities. They are complex carbohydrates and are full of fibre, so they fill you up nicely, have few calories, are delicious to eat and are full of nutrients. For those who are non-vegetarians and more physically active, a piece of fish or chicken can accompany the meal. Avoid curries because they make you eat more rice.

Dinner

The most important thing about dinner is actually the timing. I suggest you do not eat anything past 9 p.m. Ideally, dinner should be eaten by 8 p.m. Your dinner menu can be similar to the lunch menu I suggested earlier, and I strongly recommend that you have some vegetables with your meal. I always like to start with a small vegetable salad, no matter what else I eat afterwards. It is not difficult to cut some carrots, cucumbers and tomatoes. You can even add apple or pomegranate to your salad.

The Difference between Vegetarians and Non-Vegetarians

In India, we are lucky to have a wide array of vegetables and dishes that cater to vegetarians. India is probably the easiest place in the world to be a vegetarian. For vegetarians, I would say, please go the extra mile, and have two or even three vegetables for dinner. You can choose from the following:

1. Okra
2. Tinda
3. Beans
4. Carrots
5. Beetroot
6. Eggplant
7. Tomato
8. Cucumber
9. Pumpkin
10. Squash
11. Coconut
12. Broccoli
13. Cabbage
14. Cauliflower

15. Spinach
16. Green peas
17. Capsicum
18. Broad beans
19. Jackfruit
20. Ridge gourd (zucchini)
21. Drumstick
22. Chickpeas
23. Sprouts
24. Asparagus
25. Chinese cabbage
26. Snake gourd
27. Mustard greens
28. Mushroom
29. Bitter gourd
30. Radish (mooli)
31. Bottle gourd

There are many more local vegetables in India, but I have listed thirty-one, one for each day of the month. There are also foods that are not part of the Indian diet, but ought to be. These are avocados, artichokes and bamboo shoots, which can be nutritious additions to the Indian diet.

If you are non-vegetarian, by all means feel free to eat a portion of chicken/fish/prawns along with the rest of your meal, but not daily. I believe that meat should be an occasional treat for non-vegetarians, and not something they should eat every day. The reason is that meat can also be addictive, and it comes at the expense of a balanced diet. Too much of anything is bad. This is why I encourage non-vegetarians to have at least two meat-free days in a week.

I strongly recommend that diabetics should start eating eggs. I know it is difficult for Indian vegetarians to get used to the smell of eggs after a lifetime of not eating eggs, but please think of your health. Nothing beats an egg in terms of the sheer number of essential nutrients, including protein, calcium and good fats, that it contains. When buying eggs, buy the highest-quality that you can find.

The Superfoods That You Simply Should Not Live Without

Ordinarily, when I see claims about superfoods, I maintain a healthy scepticism. It usually means there is some sales pitch coming your way. I have repeatedly asserted that humans are adapted to eating a wide variety of foods, and there are many things that are good for you to eat. To my mind, superfoods are those foods that can make a tremendous positive impact on your health and well-being. Most of all, they should be cheap and widely available, and should not be made in a factory. Luckily, there are a few of these superfoods that should be an essential part of our regular diet.

Okra

Nisha was diagnosed with diabetes a few months ago. She reached out to a traditional doctor in Coimbatore, in southern India, who agreed to work with her provided she was committed to following his dietary advice. The doctor gave her a very simple regimen. He asked her to wash and cut two raw okras and put them in a glass of drinking water at night before bed. The next morning, she was to drink the contents of the glass. Within two months, Nisha was off her diabetic medication. She was astonished at this simple, yet miracle cure.

Raw okra is a potent source of soluble fibre. Nisha's main problem had been that she was suffering from a shortage of soluble fibre in her diet, which led to diabetes. This simple, cheap cure transformed her life.

Okra is a simple vegetable, but it packs a big punch. It is full of vitamins A and C, a bunch of antioxidants and the type of soluble fibre the human body loves. Okra serves as an excellent medium in the gut for beneficial bacteria, and facilitates a diverse and friendly gut ecosystem. Okra is an indispensable part of the human diet.

Guava

There is nothing healthier for breakfast than a guava. It is packed with dietary fibre, vitamin C and a nice dose of vitamins A and B and magnesium, as well as antioxidants. It may surprise you that a guava has more than twice the vitamin C of an orange. Starting your day with a guava will give your digestive system a proper workout, keep your stomach full, and provide slow-release nutrients for your body. Guavas have an alkaline effect, and reduce acidity.

Guavas also have the wonderful effect of feeding the 'coral reef' in your gut and serve as an excellent laxative, emptying your intestine and keeping the digestive machinery in top working order. If you can, eat a guava along with the seeds and skin. You can cut away some of the seeds if you must, but the skin is the most nutritious part and must be eaten.

Astringent fruits

We humans have evolved to eat a wide range of foods, more than any other animal species. Of the different tastes that are available to us, namely sweet, salty, hot, sour, bitter, astringent and umami, the one taste that we should focus on for good health is the taste we call astringent. Okra, guava, berries, and most fruits and vegetables that have a high fibre content have this astringent taste which is literally the taste of antioxidants. This taste is found in red wine too. In fruits, it is experienced as more of a dry mouth feeling, with perhaps a hint of sour or bitter.

In the West, astringent is barely recognized as a separate taste, but in Asian cooking, it is well known and highly regarded as a taste in its own right. In the traditional Indian system of medicine we call ayurveda, astringent is the most important taste, sought after for its ability to balance and rejuvenate the body. Today, scientists have identified a class of chemicals called polyphenols, which are found in berries, wine and in the skins of fruits. These polyphenols are the same as the foods we in India call astringent. There has been a lot of debate on polyphenols, and scientists are yet to conclusively agree on why they work, but they absolutely do.

There are two reasons why they are so good for you. First of all, polyphenols are actually poisonous. They are produced by plants to be part of the skin of fruits, so clearly the plant is producing them to ward off insects and birds. The less ripe the fruit, the more unpleasant its taste and the higher the amount of polyphenols. The human body does not like to retain polyphenols, which is why its molecules are rapidly processed by the body and broken down or disposed of. So it is clear that polyphenols trigger the hormesis effect which I will discuss in more detail in a later section. A low dose of this 'poison' actually heals your body and triggers a response that makes your body stronger, just like exercise. You can think of astringent foods as exercise for your innards.

The second explanation is what we can call the bio-reactor effect. When you eat fats, the strong acid in the stomach oxidizes some of these fats and creates dangerous chemicals called free radicals. Polyphenols, when eaten along with fats, stop saturated fats from being oxidized, and this neutralizes the free radicals. If this hypothesis is correct, and there is good evidence that it is, it makes sense to have a glass of wine with meat, both from a health perspective as well as from a taste perspective.

There is one more reason for eating astringent foods. Scientists are now realizing that there are certain foods that actually increase the number of brain cells, that is they cause the brain to regenerate. These are called neurogenesis foods. It turns out that astringent foods, berries, etc. are the ones that also promote brain-cell growth and better memory functioning. While the science is still new, this is yet another compelling reason for making these foods a regular part of your diet.

Nuts about nuts

A few recent studies have definitively shown that people who eat nuts regularly are healthier and live longer than people who do not. Daily nut eaters have also been found to have a lower risk of heart disease and diabetes.[38] This is astonishing. Nuts have been known to be energy dense, and many people avoid them because of their high calories. Doctors have been known to tell patients to avoid nuts because of their high fat content. But the reality is that nuts have good fat and they are in the category of superfoods. Nuts have a good amount of fibre and high amounts of good fat as well as protein. They are also an excellent source of minerals and antioxidants.

Eating the rainbow

Plants have evolved with a whole host of colours to make their ripe fruit appealing to birds and animals. Have you noticed how flowers are so colourful to encourage pollination? Yet, once fruits form from flowers, they resemble the colour of the plant itself so that the young fruits do not look conspicuous. When the fruits ripen, they again takes on a bright colour. It turns out that eating different-coloured foods is good for you. Of course, I am talking about natural colours here, not artificial colours added in a factory or kitchen. From this comes the concept of 'eating the rainbow', which literally means that we should seek out different-coloured fruits, vegetables and nuts to eat. It is also true that the brightest-coloured fruits like cherries, berries and dark grapes tend to have the best polyphenols and other antioxidants.

The J-curve of alcohol

Now here is something that might make you sit up and take notice. Science has proved time and again that drinking a little alcohol every day or regularly is very good for health.

This is true not just of red wine, but of any other alcoholic drink like beer, whisky, rum or vodka.

Clearly, the effect is not just because of the astringent compounds like resveratrol in the red wine. Apparently, alcohol itself is a superfood when consumed in moderation. We call this the j-curve because drinking alcohol in moderation lowers your risk of heart disease, high blood pressure, stroke and diabetes, but if you drink greater quantities, the positive effects go away and are replaced by negative effects like liver poisoning and other ailments.

All over India, liquor shops and liquor bottles carry signs that say 'Drinking alcohol is injurious to health'. I can soon see someone filing a public interest litigation, because this statement is totally false, and science has conclusively proven it to be false. A more accurate statutory warning would be, 'Drinking *excess* alcohol is injurious to health'.

Now, I am well aware that some of us have a tendency towards alcoholism and that it especially runs in families. If you are not a drinker, or are not able to moderate your drinking, please stay away from alcohol. But for the rest of us, the evidence is clear. Have one or two drinks each night, especially once you cross the age of forty. You will live longer and stay healthier. But for those of us who have an addiction to alcohol, stay off it completely. The advice contained in this book is no excuse to feed your addiction!

Turmeric powder

It may seem odd to mention the power of turmeric, as it is a staple of Indian cooking and we eat plenty of it in our daily diet. Turmeric contains an important antioxidant called curcumin. While turmeric has long been used in Indian medicine, Western medicine has recently woken up to its health benefits. Today, turmeric has been shown to relieve arthritis, reduce tumours in cancer patients, reduce symptoms in viral infections and treat diabetes and upset stomachs. While there is plenty of debate and ongoing research on curcumin, there is no doubt that we should eat more of it in our daily diet.

Dark chocolate

I know you are going to enjoy this one. Apparently chocolate is a superfood. It's true! The main ingredient in good chocolate, cocoa, is full of antioxidants; dark chocolate, particularly, has many benefits. Dark chocolate reduces your risk of developing blood clots, and lowers your heart disease risk significantly. It also lowers blood pressure, reduces chronic fatigue,[39] is anti-inflammatory and contains good fats. Apparently, chocolate also affects the serotonin level in the brain and improves mood. One study shows that cocoa can reverse age-related memory loss and improve cognitive functioning.[40]

Now a word of caution. All the junk that passes for chocolate is not actually chocolate; it is candy. Real chocolate is bitter, not sweet. The sweeter the product, the less cocoa it actually has. Food manufacturers have taken over the chocolate category, and are totally fooling the public. All the big brands do this. So-called milk chocolate has hardly any cocoa in it, and white chocolate actually has zero cocoa in it.

The only protection from this is to look for chocolate that contains at least 70 per cent cocoa. It has to be dark chocolate, with a high percentage of cocoa, for it to be healthy for you and count as a superfood. Unfortunately, true chocolate is very expensive. But if you can afford it as an occasional treat, I strongly recommend it.

Fermented foods

Some healthy foods you should be eating are fermented foods. The best example of a fermented food is, of course, curd or yogurt. Full-fat yogurt is one of the healthiest foods you can eat—even people with lactose intolerance can digest it. In other words, even if you cannot digest milk, you should be able to digest yogurt.

Fermented foods come in many forms. In India we have pickles, in Korea there is kimchi and in Japan, there is tsukemono, a type of pickle. All these fermented foods are strong flavoured and delicious once you acquire a taste for them. In the old days, fermentation was used to lengthen the shelf life of food.

Fermented foods are full of healthy bacteria so they add to the diversity of your gut ecosystem. The main type of fermentation is called lactic-acid fermentation. In fact, most of the so-called probiotics available in the market today are supplements that carry lactic-acid-producing bacteria.

Parvez et al., writing in the *Journal of Applied Microbiology*, say it best:[41]

Some of the beneficial effects of lactic acid bacteria consumption include: (i) improving intestinal tract health; (ii) enhancing the immune system, synthesizing and enhancing the bio-availability of nutrients; (iii) reducing symptoms of lactose intolerance, decreasing the prevalence of allergy in susceptible individuals; and (iv) reducing risk of certain cancers.

The mechanisms by which fermented foods actually benefit us are not yet fully understood by science, but the clue is found in how the human body itself ferments the food we eat in the large intestine. It is clear that many essential minerals and nutrients are made by bacteria in the gut through fermenting food. So it is only natural that fermentation outside the body is healthy for the body.

One of the main reasons I oppose probiotic supplements is that they are made in a factory. All you need to do to increase the good bacteria in your body is to eat naturally fermented yogurt, kimchi and Indian pickles. Of course, the supplement industry wants you to buy pills you can pop into your mouth, but this is no different from buying fibre supplements, vitamin supplements or mineral supplements.

The irony is that most fermented foods you buy in the store, like yogurt and cucumber pickles, are actually pasteurized to kill off their good bacteria. This turns them into nothing more than processed foods, and all the nutrient benefits are gone by the time you consume them. Today, even the bread that is made in a factory is full of artificial gluten. Instead of making bread the old-fashioned way, by naturally fermenting the dough, industrial bakers simply add extra gluten to dough and go from making dough to making bread in three hours flat. It is no wonder that more and more people are diagnosed with gluten allergies and celiac disease.

We have reached a point where we eat packaged sugar and corn products, drink sugary drinks, and eat processed foods with added salt and sugar and all vitamins, minerals, probiotics and enzymes removed. To counter the effects of this junk food, we eat probiotics, minerals, vitamins and other supplements that are also made in factories.

This is astonishing. All you have to do to gain and maintain excellent health is to eat natural food, which already has all the nutrients you need, and rid your life of any supplements.

Beans and dals

I am a big fan of beans/dals/pulses. They are full of fibre and protein and slow-release carbohydrates. They should form the core of any vegetarian diet. In India, I wish that our rice- and wheat-based diet would get replaced with a diet that has dals at its core. We can go a long way towards health by also including more beans in our diet. Some people are allergic to some types of beans, so as a category they get a bad name. But these people can always find other types of beans to grow and eat. The world today has over 40,000 types of beans available. Only a tiny fraction of these are mass produced for human consumption. What I would dearly love to see is a large expansion in the variety of beans available in the market.

India is already the world's largest producer of beans. What is needed is a focus on creating a larger variety of recipes for dal dishes. Towards that end, I recommend a book by the oddly named Crescent Dragonwagon called *Bean by Bean: A Cookbook: More than 175 Recipes for Fresh Beans, Dried Beans,*

Cool Beans, Hot Beans, Savory Beans, Even Sweet Beans!

In a largely plant-based diet, dals/beans are definitely a superfood!

Yogurt or curd

Plain yogurt, or curd, is a superfood. Make sure it is made of full-fat milk, and eat it in moderation. Also make sure it is not made in a factory with sugar and other stuff added to it. In India, we are lucky that quality full-fat milk is available everywhere. Most of us make yogurt at home, and long may that tradition continue!

Now here is some wonderful news for those of us who are lactose intolerant (including me). When milk gets fermented into yogurt, most of the lactose in milk is separated out into the watery part around the yogurt. Straining out the water removes the lactose. An even better idea than straining is to simply buy a clay pot and use it to make the yogurt (you get one for less than Rs 150). The clay pot absorbs much of the liquid containing the lactose on the inside, and evaporates it from the outside of the pot, creating a cooling effect. The result is yogurt that has less sugar, and is simply extraordinary in flavour. When you wash the pot, the lactose is simply washed away. I recommend getting two clay pots, because then you can use the second one to set the yogurt while you are still eating from the first one.

One can eat a cup of yogurt with every meal. It is full of healthy bacteria, lots of essential nutrients including protein, good fat, vitamins and calcium.

The Joy of Living and the Joy of Eating

The ancient Greek philosopher, Epicurus, taught that the purpose of philosophy was to attain a tranquil life characterized by ataraxia, which is peace and freedom from fear, and aponia, which is the absence of pain. He recommended that one should live a self-sufficient life surrounded by friends and loved ones. How many of us would disagree with this simple philosophy? Epicurus was also a believer in healthy eating. Taking pleasure from food can add quite a lot to the joy of living, and the Baby Elephant Diet specifically recommends it.

Here are the principles for healthy eating.

1. Eat more food than you normally do if you start following my approach. This is very important because if you don't increase the quantity of the food you eat, you will have a big calorie deficit, you will feel tired and cranky, and you will go back to eating junk comfort carbs.

2. If you get hungry while you are following my approach, eat. Do not starve yourself. Following my lifestyle is fun and easy and delicious. Do not deprive yourself of food.

3. You must change the composition of what you eat, while at the same time increasing the quantity of food.

4. The following foods are to be completely avoided on normal days, but you can have them for a cheat meal: rice and rice products, wheat and wheat products, cereal grains of any kind, bread and flour products, potatoes, sugar and sugar products, sugary fruits, fruit juices.

5. The only fruits you are allowed are fruits that have

much more fibre than sugar, such as guava and papaya. Vegetables that are actually fruits, e.g. tomato, avocado and eggplant, are allowed in unlimited quantities.

6. Eat fish, meat, whole eggs, slow carb vegetables like broccoli, beetroot, carrot, cabbage, cauliflower, all in unlimited quantities. Eat lentils and lots of beans if you are a vegetarian.

7. Nuts are allowed but no more than half a dozen almonds or the equivalent for a snack.

8. Beer is not allowed, and white wine is not allowed. Red wine, whisky and other spirits are allowed, in moderation.

9. Milk products, including cheese are allowed. Switch to full-fat milk, not 2 per cent milk. Remember, there is nothing wrong with eating fat under my diet.

10. Now for the fun part. You can take a day off from this diet, each week. This is very important. Choose one fixed day in the week, say Saturday, to eat whatever you like. The whole point of my diet is to have fun with it. If you want ice cream or pasta or rice or noodles, have it all on this day. Doing this means that you are not depriving yourself of anything, and that is psychologically important. Eat whatever you like, without guilt, one day a week. This reinforces another important rule—the importance of delayed gratification, not only in nutrition, but also in fitness, relationships and career success.

There are two important things to remember in our relationship with food.

First of all, get your body to where it needs to be using the Baby Elephant Diet—less than 18 per cent body fat if you are a man, and less than 25 per cent if you are a woman. This is phase 1.

Second, go into maintenance mode where you are generally eating lots of vegetables, eggs, fish and less than 25 per cent of your calories is coming from whole grains, and cut out the sugary carbs for the most part. This is phase 2.

When you are in maintenance mode, when that lovely pasta or that special dessert or that fresh croissant or that freshly squeezed juice winks at you occasionally from the dining table, just go for it and don't think twice. Life is about living, not constantly counting calories and worrying about food. The point is that you should let your body fat percentage dictate whether you are in phase 1 or phase 2.

While I was sitting in a cafe in Burgundy recently, looking at the petit déjeuner (breakfast), what stared back at me was a plate piled with croissants, scones, jam, orange juice and seductively coated sugar sticks to be dipped into the coffee. Even the yogurt was the fruit kind, with added sugar. But guess what, I am well below 18 per cent body fat at this point, after three years of my new nutrition-aware lifestyle. So, I just tucked into this bread-fest, and polished off the freshly squeezed orange juice as well. Is this going to have an adverse impact on me? Not if it is an occasional indulgence.

I did feel a bit of a sugar high afterwards, but hey, I was in Burgundy, and after breakfast I went for a long walk into the vineyards and burnt off the fast carbs. The views were amazing. Yes, you just have one life! Enjoy every minute of it, and if you look after your body, the odds are that it will pay you back with a long and healthy life.

Why Trying to Make Baked Goods With 'Healthy Flour and Ingredients' Is a Waste of Time

A friend of mine, who is a real estate builder, once gave me this amazing piece of information. Building a poor-quality home and a good-quality home cost almost the same. 'How is that possible?' I asked him. He said that the main cost of a house is construction material like cement and brick and mortar, so if you use the same amount of material, the cost is the same whether the quality of the house is good or bad. In other words, what matters in making a house is the quantity of the material, not so much the quality (of course, there are some minimum standards below which the house will fall down).

This is an insight that also applies to, believe it or not, baked goods. When it comes to consuming baked goods, which are all equally bad, what matters for health is the quantity consumed, not what they are made of. Have you ever had oatmeal cookies? How about banana bread made with flaxseed and millet flour? When you go to farmers' markets and health-food stores, you often see these kinds of 'feel good' products. But how healthy are they?

Of course, some people actually like the taste of oatmeal and millet flour and whole wheat flour. If this is the case, let taste be your guide. But do not be fooled into thinking they are healthier than regular cookies and pastries. They are not.

I have to say that I am truly torn here because, as a society, we need to do more to support sustainable farming and the entire chain of food distribution that comes with it, including those farmers' markets that sell chocolate cakes made of wheatgrass flour. There is also the fact that eating these things makes you feel better and healthier because of that warm halo effect of eating something that seems healthy.

But I must burst this bubble, because that is all it is, a bubble. By the time the oatmeal or wheatgrass flour is ground and processed, the fibre is gone. What remains is largely carbohydrate sugar. Sure, there may be a little more protein in wheatgrass flour, but it doesn't make much difference when it's still 80 per cent or more sugar.

Besides, in baked goods like cookies or puffs or cakes, there are other things to watch out for. The main culprit in baked goods is trans fat. Fat that is either hydrogenated or turns into trans fat during the cooking process, is really unhealthy and has no place in our diet, particularly after the age of thirty.

The second culprit to watch out for is sugar. This is especially true of 'low-fat' cookies and pastries, where instead of fat, sugar is added. This actually makes them far unhealthier than their full-fat versions made with butter. I have tasted real banana bread, which is absolutely delicious. I have also had banana bread made with millet flour, which tastes truly awful, but nutritionally is identical to regular banana bread.

When you are eating dessert, it is supposed to be a treat. Don't confuse the issue by eating unpleasant-tasting desserts because they are made of foods that are supposed to be healthy. Whatever the ingredients, the baking process reduces them to sugar without much fibre. The only way of dealing with dessert is to limit the quantity you eat. It is far better to take a small piece of something tasty, than to take a larger portion of something that is a poor substitute in terms of taste and is equally unhealthy.

Sugar Substitutes Are Poor Substitutes

A number of sugar substitutes have arrived in the market in recent times and are recommended for diabetics.. But the reports on these are not good. Sugar substitutes are linked to obesity because they change the microbiome in your gut.[42] Apparently, sugar substitutes increase glucose intolerance within a short period of time, which causes all sorts of metabolic disorders. This is borne out by plenty of anecdotal evidence. Just look at the people around you who use sugar substitutes. You will rarely find them in decent shape. One can argue that the reason they are using the substitutes is because they are not in good shape. But scientists have tested these products on normal individuals and found that in more than half of them, sugar substitutes changed the gut bacteria in a very negative way. Further research is being done on this, but until we know more, stay away from sugar substitutes.

The point is, one teaspoon of regular sugar in your tea or coffee is not going to make a big difference to your health, if you otherwise eat healthy food. For the sake of your quality of life, please do go ahead and have that teaspoon of regular sugar. This book is about eating healthy, but mental well-being is just as important. Even during the strictest phase of my diet, I never gave up my morning cup of tea, with one teaspoon of sugar in it.

6

Avoiding Shortcuts and Focusing on Results

The Terrible Rise of Bariatric Surgery

In the city of Hyderabad where my organic farm is located, a giant billboard greets me every time I drive down the old airport road. The billboard is an advertisement for bariatric surgery, proudly shouting out to passersby 'end your frustration', and showing an obese person with a dumbbell in his hand. In the US, the number of people having this surgery is close to 200,000 a year; in India it is in the low tens of thousands but rising rapidly, especially with advertisements like this billboard in Hyderabad.

There are several techniques in bariatric surgery, but basically what happens is that the stomach is stapled so that only a small pouch at the top of it is available for swallowing food. The small intestine is cut in half, and the bottom part of it is attached to this stapled stomach 'pouch'. The idea is to first reduce the stomach's capacity, and second to cut the amount of time food spends in the small intestine (where sugars and fats are absorbed). Initially, following bariatric surgery, there is significant weight loss, and the symptoms of diabetes disappear. But the long-term effects are unknown, some leading doctors claim.

'The way bariatric surgery is promoted as a "cure" for diabetes is unethical,' says Dr Arun Bal, a diabetic foot surgeon and former editor of the *Indian Journal of Medical Ethics*. 'It is a fairly new technique and we still don't know its long-term effects on the body.'[43]

This is a truly astonishing abuse of the human body and nature. Can you imagine the accumulated neglect of the body that gets you to a place where you need bariatric surgery in the first place? Sometimes the neglect is deliberate, but sometimes it is not. After all who wants to suffer the consequences of an extremely risky operation like bariatric surgery, where people are known to routinely die on the operating table, and where the risk of complications and side effects is over 30 per cent. To make matters worse, this is just in the short term. We simply do not know what will happen after ten or twenty years but the prognosis is not good. Once you have this surgery, you can forget about the Baby Elephant Diet. You will no longer be able to eat fibre, because your stomach won't be able to handle it. Your gut ecosystem would have turned into a swimming pool, kept clean only by chemicals. Your body will lose the ability to absorb vitamins and minerals as well, so you will have to get oral and intravenous vitamin shots. Essentially you will become a permanent patient of the healthcare system until the day you die. Can you guess in whose interest it is to get you into this state?

Fat Where It Is Not Supposed to Be Is the Most Dangerous Kind

The neglect usually starts with a growing belly, the result of what doctors call visceral fat accumulation. By location, there are two major types of fat in your body, subcutaneous and visceral. Subcutaneous simply means that the fat is under the skin and spread throughout the body. This type of fat is less harmful. Visceral or ectopic fat means that the fat is wrapped around your organs and shows up as deep inside the belly, and makes the belly look big and hard. Visceral fat is highly dangerous, and is the predominant cause of all obesity-related illnesses. The good news is that different body shapes and types have different amounts of subcutaneous fat (and women have more than men), but this doesn't have any negative health implications. On the other hand, visceral fat is largely diet and exercise related, so you can lose it more easily through diet (and gain it easily too through a poor diet).

Scientists have found that visceral fat is biologically active, meaning that fat cells produce hormones and interfere with body function, in a harmful way. We don't yet know the exact mechanism by which this happens, but it is clear that fat cells increase the production of immune-system chemicals called cytokines, which raise the amount of chronic inflammation in the body. This in turn increases the production of cortisol and bad cholesterol (LDL). What we know about visceral fat is that the less you have, the healthier you are.

The simplest measure of the levels of visceral or bad fat in your body is your waist circumference. For Indians, a man with a waistline over 37 inches (94 cm) and a woman with a waistline over 35 inches (89 cm), will have a level of visceral fat that is above the danger threshold.

So what happens if you get a 'tummy tuck' or liposuction to remove your tummy fat? This is one of the most dangerous things you can do to your body!

It turns out liposuction removes the healthy white fat, and your body replaces it with deadly visceral fat.[44] The good news is that you can get rid of visceral fat through exercise. However, liposuction should be done, if at all, along with an increase in exercise, and should not be done as an alternative to exercise. It would be best, of course, to avoid this sort of surgery in the first place, and use diet and exercise to achieve your health goals.

The Baby Elephant Diet is here to stop you from going anywhere near a surgeon's knife. At least an ounce of fibre every day will save you much pain in later years.

The Link between Strength Training and Reversing Diabetes

Insulin is produced in the pancreas and its role is to help your muscle cells absorb glucose (sugar) and turn it into energy. If you consume a lot of sugar, your body makes a lot of insulin. Over time, your body's cells become resistant to insulin, and you develop type 2 diabetes. To make matters worse, eventually your pancreas also produces less and less insulin.

When your body becomes insulin resistant, your muscles are unable to use the sugar you eat, resulting in fatigue. As a double-whammy, this sugar then goes to the liver and gets converted into body fat. Therefore, managing your insulin balance is key to avoiding or reversing diabetes, and there are only two ways of doing it naturally. The first is, of course, diet, specifically avoiding sugar. The second is strength training. Since I have talked about diet elsewhere in this book, I will discuss strength training and its impact on diabetes in this section.

The reason it takes diabetics much longer to show results from strength training is because their efficiency at driving energy into cells is so low. When normal people exercise, they lose fat quickly and gain muscle. When diabetics exercise, they just get tired faster. But luckily, though diabetics are slow starters, they make good progress over time and, if they persist, will end up far healthier than when they started strength training.

It is proven that strength training increases the receptivity of muscles to insulin, increasing their demand for glucose. Over time, strength training builds muscle, which directly improves metabolism and indirectly results in fat loss. When you are strength training, it is important to eat protein, but it is also important to eat more fat. Protein is important for building muscle, and fat provides calories for the energy that muscles need. Importantly, unlike sugar, the calories from protein and fat are low-glycemic, which means they are slowly digested and the body receives the glucose in a gradual and steady manner. This also means that insulin release is more regulated. Remember that insulin is an inflammatory hormone, so you don't want too much of it in your body. When you switch to a protein/fat diet, the insulin level gets regulated.

Cinnamon is a spice that is used in traditional ayurvedic medicine to lower blood sugar. Scientific studies have shown that cinnamon improves insulin sensitivity.[45] It is a good idea for diabetics to have a cup of cinnamon tea twice a day.

Beware of One-dimensional Health 'Experts'

Have you heard of the 'raw food' movement, which is made up of people who believe that we should eat only raw foods for health? Or how about the proponents of the Atkins diet who say we should eat no carbs at all, not even vegetables. You must have come across vegans who believe in no meat or dairy, and maybe even fruitarians who are convinced that we should eat only fruit (because doing so ensures the plant does not die). There is even the extreme category called breatharians, who believe that we can live on fresh air and sunlight alone (yes we can, for about four days, and then we will die of dehydration). What about the smoothie fans who only drink vegetable and fruit smoothies?

Let me tell you right away, all these diets are junk. Whenever someone tells you that you can eat only one or two types of food, they are simply showing their ignorance. The reality is that we humans can eat all types of foods. Just because we all need to eat fewer fast carbs and more fibre, does not mean that we forgo a balanced diet. Eat everything that you fancy, in moderation. But please understand what moderation is. Moderation is not eating one tablespoon of a hundred items in a buffet, in one meal. Moderation is not about eating only two servings of rice when everyone around you is eating four servings. Moderation is about eating the right proportions of a wide variety of foods. Moderation is eating two to four cups of vegetables, one to two cups of dal, one cup of full-fat yogurt, and a cup of rice for your main meal if you are an average man, and slightly less if you are a woman.

You should have one main meal each day, and two smaller

meals where you eat half to three-fourths of what I have just listed. If you like snacking, keep it to a minimum, and try not to store snacks in the house. Try not to eat alone, and try not to eat while watching television or reading a book. Let the mirror be your guide. Are you happy with your weight and your health? Then continue doing what you are doing. Otherwise, today is the day to start the Baby Elephant Diet.

7

Good Poisons in Our Diet

Ninety per cent of our health problems are a result of what we eat. Please understand this message carefully. What this means is that by merely altering the mix of what we eat, we can cure 90 per cent of our chronic ailments. Where does this leave doctors? The very best doctors build a relationship with you and help you prevent illness. But the problem is that doctors themselves, as a group, are some of the unhealthiest people around. Perhaps spending their entire day with sick people puts them into an illness frame of mind. More likely, doctors understand human frailty better than I do, because they see it all the time. On the other hand, I only see strength in people, and spend my time trying to motivate people to discover their own inner strength.

So if 90 per cent of chronic illnesses can be cured by correcting our eating habits, then why are people taking statins, reflux medications, vitamin supplements, diabetes medication and the like? It is because we humans look for the easy way out in everything. We want a pill that makes us look like Hrithik Roshan. Never mind that Hrithik works out in the gym for four hours a day (after all, he doesn't have a regular day job), and that he was endowed with genes that have made him attractive to begin with and have also given him the natural ability to be a good dancer, which he has refined through years of training. We want to eat all kinds of junk sugar foods, and we want a pill that will make our diabetes go away or at least 'manage it', whatever that means.

If you are ignorant about the relationship between food and health, there will always be a doctor or other health professional who will take your money, give you a pill, and let you continue to think that you can eat anything you want, anytime you want and in as much quantity, with few negative consequences.

So let me tell you something that you should have been taught, if not in secondary school, then at least in university. Take charge of your own diet. Be just 20 per cent more discerning in what goes into your mouth and you will be 80 per cent fitter and healthier. The last 20 per cent takes a lot more effort, but the first 80 per cent improvement is not that difficult. So what is the basic gyaan, or knowledge, that you should have about food? The simple answer is to identify and avoid foods that are poisonous for you.

Madhu is an active, attractive woman in her early fifties. For six months, she had been complaining of joint pains, especially in the big toe on her left foot. On some days, she could barely walk because of the pain, which to me seemed very much like gout. She came to me, desperate to get rid of this pain which she thought was due to menopause. I decided to forensically figure out what was the matter with her. First, I accompanied her to an orthopaedic surgeon, who could see nothing wrong in the foot X-ray and nothing that could explain the swelling on her foot. He was as baffled as we were, and recommended some Ibuprofen to manage the pain. Obviously, managing pain is not good enough. We have to try and cure, before we try and endure! I finally sat her down and asked her to write down her daily diet. Nothing untoward stood out in her diet. She is vegetarian, a moderate drinker, does yoga and strength training and is really impressive compared to most people in their fifties who are sedentary. So what could be the problem? She then wrote down all the supplements she was taking: calcium, vitamin B-12, vitamin D, protein in the form of spirulina.

Spirulina? Alarm bells immediately went off in my head and I told her to discontinue the spirulina. Two days later, her pain was 90 per cent gone and the swelling on her foot had disappeared. Today she is completely free of pain and swelling and has resumed dancing.

I am not against spirulina, though it might appear that way. Spirulina has many health benefits, for the majority of people. It is a protein supplement made from blue-green algae, and is really one of the best natural protein supplements available. But for about 15 per cent of people, it can be harmful. It can severely increase the inflammation level in their bodies and cause joint swelling and other symptoms. However, in 85 per cent of people, it is not only safe but a healthy alternative to animal protein. When I debate the effects of spirulina with naturopaths and other health practitioners, many of them think that I am crazy to suggest that it could be anything other than a miracle supplement. They scoff at the notion that it can actually be harmful to a segment of the population. Beware of health experts who are dogmatic and have one-size-fits-all solutions to every problem.

Understanding the root cause of the problem is extremely important for curing it. My friend Madhu could just as easily have gone to a doctor who would have prescribed strong anti-inflammatory medicine or steroids that may well have reduced her joint pain. But if she had taken the medicine, she would have created a second problem (side effects from medicine) to add to her first problem, which was an allergy to spirulina. Two wrongs rarely make a right in health. The best solution for her was to get rid of spirulina and regain her health naturally.

But how do we know what is harming us? It is easier than you think. Here is a list of common food products and how they can have a negative impact on the body:

Product	Symptoms
Milk	bloating, diarrhoea, constipation, acid reflux
Sugar	excess body fat, diabetes, blood pressure
Excess carbs	excess body fat, diabetes, blood pressure
Wheatgrass	heart palpitations
Spirulina	gout, joint and muscle pain
Wheat gluten	irritable bowel, ulcerative colitis, asthma

It is possible to be allergic to any substance, including water. Considering that more than 60 per cent of the human body consists of water, you would think that a water allergy was not possible. But it is. There are about a hundred people in the world who are allergic to it.

You will remember, from an earlier chapter of this book, that most plants are not interested in being eaten by predators. Being immobile, plants have to evolve defences and one defence is to have poisonous leaves and stems so that predators don't touch them. This is the reason why, even though there are about 300,000 known plant species, only about 20,000 are edible.

But not all of them are equally edible, some have degrees of edibility based on various factors, including individual body type, and the method of preparation. For many plant products, the simple act of cooking can turn something that is unpalatable into something delicious and digestible. Think of the humble potato and rice. Just boiling them in water can make these plant products edible.

In other cases, plants have co-evolved with their human friends in a process of domestication through natural selection, where wild and inedible species have mutated into highly nutritious versions that have become a natural part of the human diet. Two examples are almonds and bananas. Wild almonds are not only inedible, they actually contain a deadly poison called cyanide, and eating a handful of these bitter, wild almonds can kill you. On the other hand, the domestic version of the almond is one of the most nutritious nuts known to humans. As for bananas, which originated in Southeast Asia, the wild species actually contains 90 per cent seed, which means you cannot eat them. One out of ten thousand or so wild bananas is a mutant that does not contain seeds. At some point, humans discovered that they could take a wild mutant seedless banana and clone it using plant clippings, and thus the modern banana was born. In India, we are fortunate to have hundreds of varieties of bananas available for consumption, but in Europe and the US, there is only one variety called the Monte Carlo. In other words, every banana you get in the US is a clone of a single banana known as the Monte Carlo. The Americans have sacrificed diversity for an efficient monoculture. The bad consequences of this on their bodies, and on their ecosystem, are plain to see. But this book is not about castigating Americans, it is about making sure that we in India do not go down that same road.

What Makes a Poison, and How to Avoid It

'There are no poisons, only poisonous doses.'—Paracelsus

Paracelsus was a European physician of the sixteenth century, who is known for his studies in toxicology. He was a legendary healer, because he realized that medicines were nothing but poisons in small doses. It's all about the right dosage and the right quantity. Any food eaten in excess can kill you. We saw earlier how even alcohol is a superfood in moderate doses, offering excellent health benefits. What we see in society though is an excess of alcohol consumption, which is very harmful to both human and societal health.

Teenagers in London nightclubs often take a drug called MDMA, and some then drink too much water in too short a period of time. This can cause water poisoning, which can kill you. The point here is that you don't have to be allergic to something for it to kill you or hurt you… An excess of an otherwise healthy item can also be harmful to your health. If you eat about 2 kg of raw spinach, you are at risk of dying from cyanide poisoning, because spinach leaves contain oxalate, which converts into cyanide when it is ingested. The same food, spinach, which is considered to be a powerhouse of nutrients, is also deadly in high doses. However, the process of cooking removes the oxalate, so you can eat a lot more cooked spinach than raw.

Hormesis, the Amazing Cause of Good Health

Now we come to perhaps the most interesting subject of this book—a process called hormesis, which is literally the secret to living healthily to a ripe old age. This is the key to the fountain of youth, so read this chapter carefully. I touched on this subject briefly in my first book *All about Bacteria*, where I used the example of a former colleague I met in Boston after a gap of two years. In the interim, he had gone on a healthy diet and lost about 40 lb. I have known this colleague for nearly ten years, and he looked younger than when I had first met him a decade ago. Why is it that when obese people lose weight, they also appear to drop a few years from their age?

The answer seems to be a process called oxidative stress. Simply put, human cells use oxygen to create energy. This is a bit like fuel and oxygen burning to create heat energy, except in the case of cells, chemical energy is created. From a health standpoint, what is important is that this process involves the production of reactive byproducts called free radicals. Free radicals are balanced naturally in cells by antioxidant enzymes. Despite the bad reputation that free radicals have got in recent times, it is worth noting that in the cells, production of free radicals is not a bad thing. In fact, plenty of free radicals are produced by cells during vigorous exercise, but this is good for you because the body's response is to create antioxidant enzymes that neutralize the free radicals. Actually, once the body gets used to exercise, an increased level of antioxidant enzymes is continually produced, and scientists argue that this is what makes the benefits of exercise last longer than the exercise itself.

This process is called hormesis. It is a complex concept, but its basic premise is that a small amount of free radicals, such as those created by exercise, is good for the cells, because the body reacts with an increased defence mechanism which provides a greater net benefit even after accounting for fighting off the free radicals.[46]

But hormesis effect occurs not only with exercise, it can also be triggered by diet and environmental factors. In other words, eating low doses of poisons is actually good for you, because the body itself becomes stronger. Nicholas Nassim Taleb has written a book called *Antifragile* in which he refers to the effects of hormesis in different fields, and briefly touches on the human body.

In fact, there is a well-known effect called radiation hormesis, whereby low doses of radiation have been shown to increase average animal lifespans.[47] The risk is that it will lead to a rise in cancer occurrence due to cell mutation, but the lifespan of the overall population will go up. As with everything else, it is all about the dosage. Zero level of radiation causes severe immune dysfunction, and high doses of radiation are toxic. But there is an ideal range which is actually beneficial.

The reason a raw food/juice diet gives some people spectacular results is because of poison hormesis. All raw vegetables, especially leaves, are poisonous because of a plant's defence mechanisms. Plants simply do not want to be eaten by predators, including humans. But the fact is that the low doses of poisons found in raw vegetables can be really good for you. This is why many people who follow this diet actually get fitter and look younger. So is this an endorsement of the raw food/smoothie movement? Well, yes and no. The reason is that whether this diet works for you or not, and which combinations of raw foods you should juice, depends on your body type and your particular make-up. Raw spinach agree very well with some people but not with others. It is the same with any other raw vegetable. Some people can eat green chillis, others cannot even touch them with their hands. Yes, there is a raw food diet that will work for you, if you use trial and error and certain guidelines to figure out which vegetables suit you. You can't buy raw vegetables randomly, throw them in the blender and drink the concoction.

However, I am generally not in favour of drinking smoothies because the baby elephant would not approve. When you blend something into a smoothie, the fibre is gone, and that is not a good idea. It's much better to eat salads instead.

Here is a simple mantra for food:

> *If processed, it's awful;*
> *if natural, it's cool;*
> *if it comes with fibre removed,*
> *discard it, don't be fooled.*

Revealed: The Secret Mantra of Good Health

In the ancient scripture Bhagavata Purana, *there is the story of Lord Krishna as a child, who is caught eating dirt. When his mother Yashoda admonishes him to open his mouth, he obeys. His astonished mother sees that inside Lord Krishna's mouth is the entire universe.*

For those of us who have kids, it is not difficult to imagine how a mother might see a vision of the whole universe inside her child's mouth. Such is the love we feel for our children. But this story has a very real, modern and scientific colour to it. There is, in fact, a universe inside your mouth, a universe of 80 trillion bacterial cells in thousands of species. You should think of your mouth as the opening to a coral reef.

Please look up images or videos of a coral reef, if you have not seen or experienced one already, and you will get an idea of what lies within you. Each morning when I get up and look at myself in the bathroom mirror, I tell myself that I am a vessel for this incredible ecosystem that lives inside me. The health of this vessel, my body, is totally dependent on the health of the ecosystem. When I meditate, I think of my gut and its positive effect on me. This is not New Age fluff, it is actually science. You can literally influence your gut to be healthier simply by being aware of its importance.

Most of us care about our appearance to some degree or the other. We want to present a confident, pleasant and positive face to the world. Cosmetic companies make their billions feeding this desire of ours. So why not spend a minute each day appreciating our gut, where all our good health begins?

Appreciating our gut means thinking just for a second about what we are putting into our mouths. Imagine a small coral reef where someone dumps a drum of bleach into the water. Can you imagine what would happen to that ecosystem? Initially it would become as sterile and lifeless as a swimming pool. After a while, it would look like what a swimming pool would look like once you stopped adding chemicals to it; it would be taken over by unhealthy, aggressive and quite possibly dangerous bacteria.

Have you ever wondered why it is unhealthy to swim in a swimming pool that is not regularly maintained with chemicals, but it is perfectly safe to swim in a coral reef or in the village pond? It is the constant replenishing of the water in a coral reef that purifies the water and keeps it safe. This is the true power of biodiversity; the more biodiverse the environment, the safer and more benign it is. This is true of a forest, a coral reef and also your gut.

When you take a course of prescription antibiotics, they work inside your gut just like that bleach in a coral reef. Antibiotics wipe out huge swathes of your ecosystem, and what happens is that the few species of bacteria that are resistant to the antibiotics multiply. Some of them, like a bacterium called clostridium that is immune to all known antibiotics, can become deadly if it overgrows in your gut. The only way of keeping clostridium in check is to maintain your gut biodiversity. If you make one commitment today, commit to yourself that you will not use antibiotics unless they are absolutely necessary.

Please note that even today, most doctors are unaware of the dangers of antibiotics, and many doctors will prescribe them routinely, even if there is no benefit in doing so. Even in a developed country like America, estimates are that over 50 per cent of antibiotic prescriptions are unnecessary. For some illnesses like acute bronchitis, three out of four patients are prescribed antibiotics even though they serve no purpose at all.[48] In a place like India, doctors are even more trigger-happy in prescribing antibiotics. Many Indians actually get their antibiotics over the counter, even though it is illegal. Commit to yourself that you will question your doctor on the need for an antibiotic every time it is prescribed to you or your child. Commit also that you will not buy over-the-counter antibiotics. Please do not throw bleach into a coral reef, or antibiotics into your gut, without a valid medical reason for doing so.

Setting aside antibiotics, there are several other ways we routinely damage our gut. Of these, probably the biggest culprit, as discussed earlier, is eating too much sugar or sugary carbs like potatoes, white rice and processed flour. We have discussed how these spike your insulin, which then helps turn the sugar into body fat. We have also discussed how this can lead to insulin resistance (diabetes). Another side effect of all this sugar consumption is the overgrowth of a type of bacteria called firmicutes, which can cause vitamin deficiencies, thyroid problems and other illnesses. A diverse ecosystem needs a variety of food for optimal health. If you subsist on processed food and sugar carbs, the diversity in your gut will naturally decrease.

This lack of biodiversity inside your gut and the problems associated with it, are very real. Scientists have found that obese people have less biodiversity in their guts than thin people.[49] This is a staggering finding, but if you have read this book thus far, it should not surprise you at all!

You can literally think of obesity as a disease of low biodiversity of the gut. It is the human body equivalent of clear-cutting a Brazilian rainforest and planting a monoculture of corn. If you eat a diet that is largely made up of calories from these monoculture factory farms, your body's biodiversity will be damaged. Obesity is a symptom of this.

Americans have the least amount of biodiversity in their guts. It is not at all surprising that they are also the most obese people in the world.

Vitamin Supplements Are a Crutch You Only Need in Old Age

There is a basic truth in life. You should be deeply suspicious of anything that is made in a factory and comes in a box or bottle. You should have a good reason for putting anything that is processed into your body. Of course, sometimes it is unavoidable, like ketchup or mayonnaise or oils. All the evidence shows that frozen vegetables are also safe and nutritious. But what about vitamin supplements, those seemingly healthy pills that doctors dish out by the cupful?

Do you take vitamin supplements? Do you have those bottles of multi-coloured pills lying around at home that you occasionally pop into your mouth, or worse, into your child's mouth? Let me tell you something about the science of vitamins, so that you have the latest scientific thinking on this subject. Originally, the word vitamin was coined as 'vitamine' by a Polish scientist called Casimir Funk who thought they were nitrogen compounds (amines). The splendidly named C. Funk could not possibly have imagined this multi-billion dollar placebo industry that he spawned. The very word *vitamin* sounds like 'vital mineral', something so essential, a life-giving force.

And it is absolutely true. Vitamins are essential to the human diet. Most vitamins cannot be made in the body and they must be ingested through diet. The major exceptions are vitamins B and D. Vitamin B is made by bacteria in your gut. Vitamin D is made by your skin when exposed to sunlight. As for the remaining vitamins, you must get them from healthy foods. In India today, many affluent Indians are being diagnosed with vitamin B and D deficiencies, and we will touch on this later on in this section. As recently as the late 1990s, 57 per cent of children in India were vitamin A deficient, and at risk of developing night blindness. This situation is now vastly improved because nutrition among the poor in India is much better than it was twenty years ago.

What about vitamin C, the vitamin that marketers and mothers love, that is found in orange juice and in chewable pills, and can help ward off colds. You may recall studying about the disease scurvy, which occurs when we don't take enough vitamin C. It was only in 1753 that a Scottish scientist figured out that lemons and limes could cure and prevent scurvy. Hence British sailors were known by the derogatory term 'limey' for the lime rations they were required to take along.

Vitamin C is very important for health, no doubt. But oranges and lemons are not the best way of getting this vitamin. Guavas have far more of it, and are far healthier for you. A green pepper has a lot more; so do broccoli and cauliflower. It is clear that this essential vitamin has been taken over by the citrus industry for marketing purposes, and for peddling sugary orange juice to children.

Given all these facts, what could be the problem with eating vitamin pills every day? Quite a lot, as it turns out. First of all, vitamins are poisonous in high doses. A 100-gm dose of vitamin A can kill an adult, and 30 gm can kill a child. Even if you don't die, you could end up with a whole lot of symptoms like diarrhoea, nausea, vomiting, heartburn, abdominal cramps, headache, insomnia and kidney stones from vitamin poisoning. Second, there is now evidence that the body begins to rely on these vitamins and stops its natural methods of absorption from food. Gut bacteria, which make vitamin B, can also stop doing so if you are getting it from supplements. Third, people are notoriously inconsistent with supplements. Taking them occasionally is worse than not taking them at all. Fourth, people who take vitamin supplements use this as an excuse to eat badly. The truth is that if you are eating a varied and balanced diet, you don't need supplements. It is best to get your vitamins from natural foods, fruits, vegetables, nuts and eggs, and if you are a non-vegetarian, from fish and meat.

Health guru Dean Ornish calls vitamins brown urine generators, and he is right. What vitamins do, and do well, is to make your urine dark. Take a multivitamin pill and see what happens, if you doubt me.

There is one big exception to my rule of 'no vitamins'. If you are over sixty years old, a daily multivitamin (without iron) may be helpful, because your body's ability to absorb vitamins goes down with age. The reason is that you produce less stomach acid as you get older. Even in this case, I would argue that you are better off taking stomach acid tablets (HCL) than taking vitamins. Doctors write to me occasionally and complain that vitamins are useful for people who are on acid reflux medication or statins, and therefore suffer from poor absorption of vitamins from food. To them, my response is this: stop prescribing acid reflux medication or statins. Do not take poisons (excess vitamins) to counter the effects of other poisons (statins, acid regulators) that you are taking.

One doctor recently wrote to me and complained that he finds it quite useful to prescribe vitamins because 'they are harmless and they make people feel good'. This is quite an astonishing argument, really. What this doctor is saying is that he is supporting the placebo effect. The placebo effect is a well-known phenomenon, where patients feel good no matter what pill they take. We have an entire branch of medicine called homeopathy that is dedicated to the placebo effect, so why do we need allopathic doctors to do this? There is no evidence that multivitamins are useful for healthy people below sixty, so doctors should stop promoting them. More importantly, doctors have a responsibility to suggest natural remedies such as a healthy vegetable-filled diet, and not shortcuts like supplements. Luckily, this is starting to happen, at least in some places. At Harlem medical centre in New York and a few other hospitals in the US, there is a fruit and vegetable prescription programme that doctors are actively prescribing to families with obesity problems.[50]

Having said this, two of the most common health issues I see today in people over thirty-five, are deficiencies of vitamin B and vitamin D. In fact, this is the first thing I look for when assessing people in my preventive health programme. One of the easiest ways of improving health is to cure deficiencies of these vitamins.

Vitamin B actually refers to eight different vitamins that are generally found together in food (collectively called B complex). Vitamin B12 cannot be made by plants or animals; only bacteria can synthesize it. A host of organisms in the human gut have the capability of making B12 for the body's needs. Vitamin B5 is also made in the gut and absorbed through the lining of the gut.[51] Generally, as we get older, our ability to make or absorb vitamin B goes down, so we need to take extra care to get enough of it. Indian vegetarians are especially vulnerable while non-vegetarians can get enough vitamin B from meat, poultry and eggs. If you have unexplained chronic pain, especially in the feet, it is worth looking at your vitamin B profile.

It is quite remarkable that vitamin D deficiency is one of the most common conditions affecting us. After all, the sun shines all day, and vitamin D is made by our body when it is exposed to sunlight.Vitamin D deficiency leads to heart disease, high blood pressure, diabetes and all the familiar immune illnesses.[52] This deficiency is also totally preventable.

The most important way of getting your vitamin D is by being out in the sun with exposed skin. If you are fully covered up, that will not help. What I recommend is that you wear shorts and sit out in the sun for a cup of tea. The best way is to sit half in the shade and half in the sun, so that your upper body is comfortably cool in the shade, and your legs are out in the sun. Just do this with a cup of tea and a newspaper in your hand each morning or afternoon, and you are set to live a long and healthy life.

8

Healthy Eating in Simple Steps

Six Simple Habits That Can Permanently Change Your Health for the Better

So what are the steps to healthy eating? Here are the six steps to get you started:

Resolve that you will try to avoid eating directly from a plate. Use small bowls instead.

When you use a plate, you are essentially using rice or chapathi as a binding agent, to hold the food, add bulk and ship it to your mouth. These binding agents are not necessary at all, and are the cause of all our weight and health problems. Get rid of them, or cut them down by 90 per cent. You can't eat dal on a plate, so you end up putting in rice, building something like a Bhakra Nangal dam to hold the dal on your plate, and then you eat both the dal and rice. Dal is healthy, but rice is not. So just eat the dal...in a bowl. Eat vegetables, eggs, yogurt, pickles, all from small bowls. When you switch from a plate to small bowls, you automatically cut down on your consumption of rice and chapathis. The spice levels in your food will also fall, because you are no longer eating bland rice or chapathis with other food items. Most of us would not touch a bowl of rice on its own, so we overspice other food items and then mix them with bland rice and eat them. Just cut the rice out. Enjoy the vegetables on their own. They are delicious and healthy.

Get smaller spoons and bowls.

There is a simple way of fooling the brain into believing that you have eaten plenty of food even if you haven't: use smaller spoons and bowls when you eat. This has been confirmed by numerous studies that show that we are totally incapable of judging how much food we eat. One famous study,[53] titled 'Lessons from the Bottomless Bowl', tested people with bowls of soup that were automatically refilled through a hole at the bottom of the bowl. Another group of volunteers had soup from regular bowls. The people whose bowls were refilled, ate 73 per cent more soup, but did not believe they had done so. Even more astonishing, both sets of volunteers reported feeling the same level of satiation.

The lesson from this is clear. You will automatically eat less if you use smaller bowls and plates. Using a smaller spoon also helps when eating ice cream or other treats.

Be careful about who you spend your time, and especially your meals, with.

It is worth repeating what Jim Rohn, an American motivational speaker, once said, 'You are the average of the five people that you spend your time with.' It is a very interesting observation, and has a ring of truth to it. When you see smokers bunched outside, lighting away, you can see this in action. Not just smokers, obese people stick together, unhealthy people stick together and fit people stick together. If your core support network is a group of people whose dietary habits are terrible, then you are going to have a real problem breaking out of this. You can be as disciplined as you like, but if you then go to your best friend's house and eat 'Unhealthyram namkeen', then all your discipline and change in lifestyle will come to nought.

Do not mix eating with another activity.

Do you like watching TV while eating? Or do you eat while watching TV? Or do you read a book while eating? Stop doing other activities while eating. Eating time should be reserved for eating. You will totally lose track of what and how much you are eating if you are distracted. Eat your food slowly, enjoy and savour it. If you like, have a conversation with someone while eating, but don't read or watch TV.

Always eat the fibre first.

The sequence of the foods you eat can have a big impact on your health. Starting a meal with soup is a terrible idea. The soup is a mechanically processed liquid (home blending is still processing), whose sugar content gets rapidly absorbed by your digestive system, especially when you are hungry. What you need to do is to start the meal with the most fibrous vegetable. Along with it, eat the protein which is harder to digest, so that it gets doused in that initial stomach acid bath. Fibre and protein also fill you up and make it less likely that you will overeat. Eat the soup last or not at all. I rarely eat soup, unless it is full of vegetables packed with fibre.

Avoid drinking your calories.

The best drink is water, plain and simple. Drink it to your heart's content and no more. Juices are really bad for you, so are fizzy drinks and beer is a sugar bomb. Avoid, or minimize, these. Definitely no buttermilk! Buttermilk is a marketing term for butter-less milk. I have never figured out why the authorities allow manufacturers to call yogurt water with its butter removed, buttermilk. It should be called what it is, butter-less milk. Butter-less milk is basically sugar water with a bit of protein. No need to put that into your body at all. Fruits are fine to eat, but avoid watermelon and grapes which are basically sugar bombs with no fibre.

The Vegetarian Guide to Healthy Eating

This book is about nutrition and not about the ethical choices involved in what we eat. I am here to educate you in simple terms about what the human body can eat and what the human body can cope with. The decisions regarding your food choices are pretty much yours, but you should start with a framework that is science-driven, and then you are welcome to add layers of emotion (I won't eat X because it tastes bad) or religion (I won't eat Y because my faith prohibits it) or ethics (I won't eat Z because I am ethically opposed to how it is grown).

The framework is quite simple. Our planet is a biosphere. No parts of the planet's surface or ocean depths, where sunlight reaches either directly or indirectly, are entirely without life. Scientists have found living ecosystems on remote Antarctica and even in the deepest ocean; wherever there is warmth, there is life. Entire ecosystems live and thrive on volcanic vents in the deep ocean. There are over ten million species of microbes on our planet, and most are adapted to very specific environments with regard to temperature, oxygen levels and moisture.

Closer home and to our food, only 1 per cent of soil microbes have been identified thus far,[54] but it's clear that without microbes, soil would be dead and no plant growth would be possible. One square metre of soil contains 10 trillion bacteria, 10 billion protozoa, 5 million nematodes, 100,000 mites, 50,000 springtails, 10,000 animals known as rotifers and tardigrades, 5,000 insects and spiders, 3,000 worms and 100 snails, according to biologist James Nardi.[55] Lots of rats (which are mammals) are killed during the mechanical harvesting of rice or wheat. Plants themselves have a certain amount of 'intelligence' or sentience, even though this theory is highly contested today.

The ethical basis of veganism boils down to the principle of least harm. Eating always involves taking life, whether it is plant life or animal life. The least harm principle says that because we would die if we did not eat, we are obligated to eat in a way that causes the least harm to other life. In the sentient hierarchy of life, each species has a place and animals are above plants in sentience and their ability to feel pain and suffering. Also, each pound of animal flesh requires many pounds of plants. Given these two facts, it makes sense to eat only plants, according to vegan philosophy.

In India, some 40 per cent of people are vegetarians, but we happily consume milk and milk products while turning a blind eye to the appalling conditions in many dairy farms. But the real suffering to animals happens in factory farms, especially in the US where chickens and cows are treated like objects and go through enormous suffering in their short lives before they are turned into meat products.

I have nothing against people's food choices, but I do want everyone to be aware of where their food is coming from. I have come to a point where I am conscious of the love that has gone into preparing the food that I am eating. If someone cooks my food while they are in a bad mood or in a stressful state, I can feel the difference in taste. Similarly, if the food itself contains flesh from animals that suffered all their lives, the food tastes rancid in my perception.

Given this, I no longer eat factory-farm products, especially meat. This means that functionally I am a vegetarian. I have access to milk from a small farm that treats its buffaloes quite well, so I do consume milk products. I also eat eggs, but these come from my own farm, where all my girls (giriraja and vanaraja and country hens) are treated like rock stars and have lots of space to roam. My approach is pragmatic, ethical and driven by revulsion to factory farming as well as a new-found spirituality. I do recognize that not everyone has access to ethical sources of animal products, so I leave it to you to decide how you resolve the ethical issues.

Let us recognize that every day we are making lifestyle decisions that have a negative impact on the environment.

Taking airplanes, driving a car, using an air conditioner, eating meat, these are all bad for the environment. But if we can be conscious of this and work towards creating a positive impact on our environment in other ways, then we can still live well and save the planet for future generations. Meat should be an expensive and occasional treat if it is a part of your diet. Do try and make sure it is ethically sourced if you are going to eat it.

There is another huge benefit of my approach. Whoever follows it will be healthier, because they will automatically reduce their meat consumption by 90 per cent or more.

How to Cure Diabetes with This Delicious Diet

You probably have a close family member or friend who has diabetes. Yes, it is that common, this deadly disease affecting one in four of us as we age. Type 2 diabetes is fundamentally a disease of neglect of our bodies over decades, not just years.

You see, diabetes is something I call the default illness. If it runs in your family, then you too will get it by default. That does not mean that it is your family's fault. We like to blame our genes, but genes are just a blueprint, they are not destiny. If you know that it runs in your family, should you not be extra careful, starting at age thirty-five?

This book will give you the tips and tools for preventing diabetes, and if you already have it, you will learn how to reverse it. Yes, it is possible, in most cases, to reverse diabetes. But the longer you have had it, the harder it is to reverse it. Most of the medical community, and even many nutritionists, will tell you that diabetes is a lifelong chronic condition and should be managed. What they actually mean is that given the decades of neglect that got someone into this situation in the first place, chances are that person is not now going to put in the effort to change their habits and reverse the curse.

But I am not that kind of counsellor. If you are okay consuming pills to manage this disease, and with the slow but inevitable progression to injecting insulin, losing your sense of sight, hearing, feeling and sexual pleasure, and eventually becoming an invalid, then I am not the guide for you.

The Twelve-step Guide to Reversing Diabetes

1. Start with a full diagnostic health check-up. Keep a note of what your numbers are on diabetes and cholesterol.

2. The number one objective is to lose body fat. Eliminate grains from your diet today. This initial period of no grains and sugars will last three months to a year or more, depending on how overweight you are.

3. Eliminate all liquid calories. No juices, no sugary drinks, no alcohol.

4. Replace the grains with fibre, which means eat more vegetables like beans, cabbage, cauliflower, broccoli, peppers, eggplant, okra, tinda, mushrooms, and avocados. Eat more fruit like guavas, papaya, pomegranate, and whole oranges.

5. Eat your food in small bowls. Get rid of plates.

6. Increase the amount of food you eat. Yes, increase it! This is not a starvation diet. Remember that a cup of rice is 220 calories and a cup of spinach is 15

calories. So if you eliminate grains, you have to eat more vegetables. Also eat more protein.

7. At the same time, embark on a strength-training programme. Strength training is the only other way of reducing insulin resistance and increasing insulin sensitivity (other than diet). When you do strength training in conjunction with a good diet, the effect is multiplied. Your objective should be to add at least 5 kg of muscle in a year. Forget your daily walk (brisk or not). Hire a trainer who can promise you 5-kg muscle gain in a year, and reward the person with a big bonus when you reach that goal.

8. Contrary to what you may have heard, yoga does not reverse diabetes.

9. Take a course in pranayama (yogic breathing). If you practice pranayama regularly, your food cravings will reduce, your blood pressure will become regulated, your stress levels will go down and your insulin resistance will also go down. This is a crucial step for reversing diabetes.

10. Every two months you must have a blood test to keep track of your progress. The worse your diabetes, the more important this is. It is also important because if you follow this guide, as you start losing fat from your body, your dosage of diabetes medication—metformin and insulin—will come down. It is important to monitor this and work with your doctor to lower the doses of these chemicals as your body improves.

11. Eventually, your intake of diabetes chemicals should go down to zero. Your body shape will change, your

energy levels will be high and constant throughout the day, and you will have no food cravings.

12. If you have got this far, congratulations! If you have not, do not give up hope. Typically, my mentees have multiple false starts before they succeed. Just keep trying and you will succeed too.

Conclusion

The baby elephant is a great motivator, which is why Ganesha is the god of new beginnings. Don't wait for the new year, and don't wait for an opportune day to start this new diet. Go to the nearest mirror right now, take a hard look at yourself and promise that you will treat your body like a temple this day onward.

Here is a checklist of what the baby elephant says about eating habits that will radically change your health for the better.

1. The baby elephant eats lots and lots of fibre. This is perhaps the most crucial piece of advice in this book. Start your day with a good dose of fibre—I am talking about vegetable or fruit fibre. Guava, papaya, Chinese vegetables, broccoli, are just some of the nutrient-packed foods that are also full of good fibre.

2. The baby elephant has a nose that extends three feet long. Obviously you do not, but what I mean here is that scientists have proven that 80 per cent of our tasting sensation comes from our noses. In other words, you can get 80 per cent of the satisfaction from a food just from the smell, without eating it. One of my

greatest pleasures is walking through a street market in different parts of the world and just smelling the variety of foods cooking. Best of all, this experience is completely free of cost! But keep that three feet distance from the food you smell.

3. The baby elephant has very thick skin. Of course it does; it is an elephant. But what this means for you is that you have to change the way you think about food and go against all the established Indian social norms. Do not let anyone dictate what goes into your mouth. Resist all attempts from family and friends to feed you junk sugar or junk carbs. Cleaning your plate to avoid 'wasting food' is the worst habit of all. This is something that is drilled into us as children, but as adults it is a terrible idea to put something into your mouth just because it will 'go waste' otherwise. Your mouth is not a garbage bin! The biggest waste of all is when you eat something that you don't need to or don't want to eat.

4. The baby elephant has great presence and charisma. Have you ever looked at a baby elephant and not smiled? The sight of a baby elephant evokes positive feelings in your mind. If Ganesha showed up at an office tomorrow and asked for a job or a raise, which boss would refuse him? When you follow the Baby Elephant Diet, you will end up with a body that is stunning. Your personal charisma and confidence will get a boost and you will enjoy greater professional and personal success.

There are plenty of diet books available, with a new one being written every week somewhere around the world. But there is a huge amount of misinformation out there, largely driven by vested interests for commercial gain. Even the best nutritionists in India are selling you some totally bogus supplements to make money. Your health is not their priority, making money is. On the other hand, there are some excellent ayurvedic and homeopathic doctors who really are interested in your health and wellness. These people do not get to build palatial homes in the best localities, because they are not money-minded. This book is dedicated to them, my gurus, who are the real vaidyas.

In the end, we are responsible for our own health. Ninety per cent of health is in the mind, and any good healer knows this. I am a health mentor to many people, and most of them are very smart and successful people. The first thing I look for is a mental block, some sort of issue in their life that is causing stress, which shows up as a physical ailment. So my work with my mentees tends to be very personalized, because everyone has a different issue that shows up as ill health. My methods always involve strengthening the body, mind and spirit. When done right, this tends to have a magical effect on people's health.

To my readers I would say, look within yourself for answers to your health problems. You will find the answers there most of the time, but if you are not able to, don't worry. Find an ayurvedic practitioner or a good homeopath. These doctors treat stress very well, and the underlying condition then usually disappears.

Fond wishes and good health!

Ravi Mantha

Appendix I

Why We Are Like Mosquitoes: A Reality Check for Vegans

This book is titled *The Baby Elephant Diet*, and the reason for the title is that I want you, my dear readers, to broadly emulate the elephant in the diet department—eat more fibre and have a predominantly vegetarian diet.

But let us not lose sight of the fact that humans are not, in fact, elephants. For one thing, an elephant needs to eat between 140 and 270 kg of food every day, which is the same as the body weight of two to four adult humans. If you need any proof that what matters for health is not how much you eat but the quality of the food you eat, this should resolve all your doubts. But the point is that elephants are herbivores and humans are omnivores.

Now I want to give you a small example showing the power and balance of nature. Have you ever wondered why only female mosquitoes bite animals? How do the males survive? They live on plant sap. How can you have a species where one sex is vegetarian and the other is non-vegetarian? The answer is actually very simple. All mosquitoes live on plant sap, both male and female. In other words, mosquitoes are predominantly vegetarians. The reason female mosquitoes need a blood meal is because there is a particular protein food found only in animal blood that mosquitoes need for laying eggs. It is quite remarkable because this makes mosquitoes dependent on hard-to-obtain blood for propagating themselves. If you take away the animals, mosquitoes will simply live out their lives on plant sap and die without reproducing. This is actually nature's way of creating a dependence between otherwise unrelated species.

But why would nature create this dependence? The mosquito is one of the oldest species of insects. Would it not have been better if mosquitoes had evolved not to need blood meals? Well, think of a scenario where mosquitoes did not need blood. Given that each mosquito can lay 250 eggs at a time and can do this multiple times over her lifespan, it would not take long for the entire planet to be completely overrun by mosquitoes, until every plant was sucked dry. Actually, there are some species of mosquitoes that do not feed on blood. Instead, they feed on the larvae of other mosquitoes, so their survival depends on bloodsuckers and indirectly on animal blood.

The point of this example is to illustrate something very important. Humans are a bit like mosquitoes in this regard, in that they cannot survive and reproduce without animal products. Sorry vegans! I am here to tell you that all available science so far shows that veganism is insufficient for humans, who are omnivores, to survive.

Sorry Maneka Gandhi! While I deeply sympathize with the plight of animals held and tortured in appalling conditions in dairies, factory farms, feedlots, etc., there is today simply no alternative to consuming animal products. Perhaps in our lifetime we will be able to grow milk and meat artificially in commercial quantities, and I strongly support such research. We should do everything we can to minimize animal suffering, as long as we ensure the human race survives.

Vegan societies have never survived through human history. Today's vegans suffer from a wide variety of nutritional deficiencies, health problems, reproductive ailments and diseases. The longer you are a vegan, the more you suffer. Luckily, Indian vegetarians are a different breed altogether (except for Manekaji's followers who are vegans). We define ourselves as vegetarian but happily eat milk and milk products. The good news is that you can survive on a largely vegetarian diet as long as you consume milk products. But make no mistake, being an Indian 'pure vegetarian' is no different from that variety of mosquito that does not directly suck blood but depends on eating the larvae of other bloodsucking mosquitoes.

My point is not to scare you into removing dairy from your diet. Quite the opposite. In fact, I am here to tell you, again, that you cannot survive and reproduce and maintain good health without consuming animal protein. But be aware that eating always involves harming plants and animals. The main thing is to reduce the harm to a minimum.

I am a health writer. My starting point is that I want you to enjoy the best of health and longevity. The treatment of animals and other species is to me secondary to preserving human health. Science teaches me that humans are designed to be omnivores (sort of like mosquitoes) in order to ensure the survival of the species, and there is nothing we can do at this point to change it. We can only hope that technology will provide a solution in the coming decades.

Vegans are very decent people. They start with the premise that animals are sentient and so we should not harm them. Vegans are prepared to change their diet to make this happen, regardless of the consequences to themselves and their health.

Where I totally agree with vegans is that factory farming not only involves excessive suffering of animals, but also the quality of meat raised from factory farms is likely to do us more harm than good over the long term. This is a dilemma! We need meat and dairy, but the way much of these products are produced today is distressing. What do we do?

For starters, we can all lobby for stringent regulation of factory farms. This means the price of meat and eggs and milk will double, but so be it. Although we need these products, we don't need large quantities of them. Recently, American chicken products have been allowed into India by the World Trade Organization (WTO). This is a terrible idea, because the Americans are notorious for animal suffering and they invented factory farms in the first place. What they will now do is dump their cheap antibiotic-filled chickens into India and force our poultry farmers to use the same methods to grow our chickens in order to compete.

Instead, we should come up with ethical standards for poultry and dairy and incorporate them into WTO rules. That way, only firms (including American ones) that follow our standards of animal ethics will be allowed to sell in India.

Appendix II

Sustainable Farming and Nutrition: The Real Answers

Before I wade into the emotional ocean that is animal rights and nutrition ethics, let me tell you at the outset that I am very much committed to the ethical treatment of animals. Factory farming is the worst blight that has been inflicted on this planet and we will see nature fighting back in the next few decades. Animals are treated appallingly by the factory-farm industry, and this must change. Animal welfare is important. Humans cannot prosper while we turn away from the suffering of creatures that are closer in sentience to us than to oysters.

I use oysters for this analogy here because the most objective ethicists in the world generally agree that an oyster is okay to eat even for vegans, and that its level of sentience is too low for us to worry about it. I also do so because most of us would put oysters firmly in the animal kingdom, in their shape, texture and taste.

The flag-bearer of the vegan and animal ethics movement, Peter Singer, has gone back and forth on this, but now says oysters and species with lower sentience than oysters are okay to eat even for strict vegans. If you are a cultural vegetarian, you might find this surprising, but please understand that vegetarianism drawing on culture or religion or a strict definition of plant versus animal is not the same as using animal ethics and sustainability ethics to come up with a definition. The debate, of course, continues, but I am talking here about logic-driven ethics, not emotion-driven ethics.

Every living creature has sentience, if you describe sentience as 'response to stimulus', including the 90 trillion bacterial cells that live in and on your body. Obviously, sentience is a continuum and we have to draw the line somewhere, and most logical ethicists and philosophers draw it at molluscs like scallops and oysters. Eating ethics itself is a continuum. Some people draw the line at plants, others at milk and eggs, still others at fish, others at cows and pigs, still others at dogs and primates. All of us draw the line at cannibalism.

The fundamental problem is that humans must consume some animal protein to reproduce. I do not state this as a fact, but as an extremely strong hypothesis. Given that there have never been vegan societies in human history, it seems highly likely that without animal protein, we cannot reproduce beyond one or two generations. So we cannot give up milk products at least. I believe that ethically sourced eggs are also vegetarian, and eating eggs of free-range chickens will keep you strong and healthy. But, as I showed earlier, the ethics, as opposed to the cultural acceptability, of consuming milk is not different from that of eating meat in terms of animal welfare (most ethicists would actually argue that in factory farming, meat animals suffer less than milk animals), especially since most milk comes from factory farms.

So what are we to do? I don't necessarily have an answer for you, but I have an answer for myself. I have bought farmland, and I am growing food for myself and for 500 of my closest friends and their families. I am also rearing my own animals for milk and eggs, and my animals are free-range and are treated extremely well.

Now here is the broader issue. The argument that some vegetarians make that you can grow lots more plants than animals on a given piece of land is misguided. They are technically correct, but only until you consider that you are using massive amounts of fossil fuel and artificial fertilizers and are degrading the soil in order to grow plants using factory-farming methods. This works for a while, but is not sustainable.

The way one should look at the problem is this:

What is a sustainable ecosystem that one can have on a piece of land that is biodiverse, sustainable, protects the soil, is carbon-neutral and still generates a surplus of food, both plant and animal?

Farmers, including me, who practise permaculture, look at the world in this way. Realistically, I don't believe that we can feed seven billion people, let alone twelve billion, with these methods, although my readers can definitely afford to pay a bit more for their food to be produced sustainably. I do believe that technological advancement will make it possible to increase biodiversity and feed the world at the same time, but we need to spend a lot more on research and development. This is where I believe India can show the way, because animal ethics and biodiversity are deeply embedded in our sanatana dharma (eternal set of duties). We do have to update our ethics for the twenty-first century, but that should not be too difficult.

We must resist at all cost the factory-farming industrial complex. Factory farms have indeed solved the problem of world hunger temporarily, but at the enormous cost of planetary destruction, and their solutions destroy the land and are not sustainable.

My previous health book, *All about Bacteria*, talked about the biodiversity of the human body and the various species of bacteria and other creatures that live on us and inside us. The focus of that book was on how good health depends on a high degree of biodiversity. What applies inside our body also applies outside, in nature. Biodiversity is good everywhere, and attempts to reduce it are always unsustainable and doomed to failure.

This book is mainly about human nutrition, but good health always comes from sustainable practices, so I urge you to keep your eyes open and find sustainable food and pay a bit more for it. Choose your food well, for your children's inheritance (of this planet and its bio-resources) depends on it.

Endnotes

1. M.G. Kulovitz, et al., 'Potential role of meal frequency as a strategy for weight loss and health in overweight or obese adults', *Nutrition*, April 2014, 30(4):386-92. DOI: 10.1016/j.nut.2013.08.009. Epub 2013 Nov 20. http://www.ncbi.nlm.nih.gov/pubmed/24268866

2. http://www.huffingtonpost.com/2012/11/07/drunken-elephants-ransack-indian-village_n_2089483.html

3. http://www.sugar.org/sugar-your-diet/family-health/glycemic-index/

4. http://oddculture.com/weird-news-stories/the-fat-fiancees-of-africa/

5. Aimee Groth, 'You are the average of the five people you spend the most time with', 24 July 2012, http://www.businessinsider.com/jim   rohn-youre-the-average-of-the-five-people-you-spend-most-time-with-2012-7#ixzz 3g9g7BXDK.

6. http://www.sott.net/articles/show/242516-Heart-Surgeon-Speaks-Out-On-What-Really-Causes-Heart-Disease

7. http://classes.ansci.illinois.edu/ansc438/milkcompsynth/milkcomp_vitamins.html

8. M.I. Kratz, T. Baars, S. Guyenet, 'The relationship between high-fat dairy consumption and obesity, cardiovascular, and metabolic disease', *European Journal of Nutrition*, February 2013, 52(1):1-24. DOI: 10.1007/s00394-012-0418-1. Epub 2012 Jul 19. http://www.ncbi.nlm.nih.gov/pubmed/22810464

9. http://edition.cnn.com/2010/HEALTH/11/08/twinkie.diet.professor/index.html

10. http://www.redorbit.com/news/science/1112648268/scientists-find-gene-behind-ripe-tasteless-tomatoes/

11. Marion M. Lee, Shirley Huang, 'Immigrant women's health: nutritional assessment and dietary intervention', *The Western Journal of Medicine*, August 2001, 175(2): 133–7. PMCID: PMC1071509http://www.ncbi.nlm.nih.gov/pmc/articles/PMC1071509/

12. Ying Bao, Jiali Han, Frank B. Hu, Edward L. Giovannucci, Meir J. Stampfer, Walter C. Willett, and Charles S. Fuchs, 'Association of nut consumption with total and cause-specific mortality', *New England Journal of Medicine*, November 2013, 369: 2001-11. 10.1056/NEJMoa1307352 http://www.nejm.org/doi/full/10.1056/NEJMoa1307352

13. http://www.bbc.com/news/health-19545697 10-sep-2012

14. C.W. Cheng et al., 'Prolonged fasting reduces IGF-1/PKA to promote hematopoietic-stem-cell-based regeneration and reverse immunosuppression', *Cell Stem Cell*, 5 June 2014, 14(6): 810-23. DOI: 10.1016/j.stem.2014.04.014.
http://www.ncbi.nlm.nih.gov/pubmed/24905167

15. Diane E. Threapleton, Darren C. Greenwood, Charlotte E.L. Evans, Cristine L. Cleghorn, Camilla Nykjaer, Charlotte Woodhead, Janet E. Cade, Chris P. Gale and Victoria J. Burley, 'Dietary fibre intake and risk of first stroke—A systematic review and meta-analysis' *Stroke*, 28 March 2013. DOI: 10.1161/STROKEAHA.111.000151

16. http://www.medicalnewstoday.com/articles/217081.php

17. http://www.nature.com/nm/journal/vaop/ncurrent/full/nm.3444.html

18. Jennifer L. Pluznick, et al., 'Olfactory receptor responding to gut microbiota–derived signals plays a role in renin secretion and blood pressure regulation', *Proceedings of National Academy of Sciences*. Published online before print 11 February 2013. DOI: 10.1073/pnas.1215927110;http://www.pnas.org/content/early/2013/02/05/1215927110

19. S.I. Liu, W.C. Willett, J.E. Manson, F.B. Hu, B. Rosner, G. Colditz, 'Relation between changes in intakes of dietary fibre and grain

products and changes in weight and development of obesity among middle-aged women', *American Journal of Clinical Nutrition*, November 2003, 78(5):920-7.http://www.ncbi.nlm.nih.gov/pubmed/14594777

20. Michael Pollan, 'Some of my best friends are germs', *The New York Times Magazine*, 19 May 2013, http://www.nytimes.com/2013/05/19/magazine/say-hello-to-the-100-trillion-bacteria-that-make-up-your-microbiome.html?pagewanted=all&_r=0

21. http://ukpmc.ac.uk/abstract/MED/10340798/.0

22. http://www.businessinsider.com/jim-rohn-youre-the-average-of-the-five-people-you-spend-the-most-time-with-2012-7

23. http://blog.zocdoc.com/are-egg-yolks-bad-for-you-fact-vs-myth/

24. http://www.nytimes.com/2012/06/03/opinion/sunday/we-only-think-we-know-the-truth-about-salt.html?pagewanted=all

25. U. Smith, 'Dietary fibre, diabetes and obesity', *International Journal of Obesity*, 1987, 11 Suppl 1:27-31. //www.ncbi.nlm.nih.gov/pubmed/ 3032822

26. A.T. Erkkilä, A.H. Lichtenstein, 'Fiber and cardiovascular disease risk. How strong is the evidence?', *Journal of Cardiovascular Nursing*, January–February 2006, 21(1): 3–8. http://www.ncbi.nlm.nih.gov/pubmed/16407729

27. Valarie Burke et al., 'Dietary protein and soluble fiber reduce ambulatory blood pressure in treated hypertensives', *Hypertension*, 2008, 31:821–6. http://hyper.ahajournals.org/content/38/4/821.full

28. http://news.discovery.com/human/health/yawning-social-behavior.htm

29. Eric Robinson and Suzanne Higgs, 'Food choices in the presence of "healthy" and "unhealthy" eating partners', *British Journal of Nutrition,* 2013, 109:765-71. DOI:10.1017/S0007114512002000. http://journals.cambridge.org/action/displayAbstract?aid=8836217&fileId=S0007114512002000

30. http://blogs.scientificamerican.com/guest-blog/2014/06/12/what-does-mindfulness-meditation-do-to-your-brain/

31. http://www.newyorker.com/reporting/2009/05/18/090518fa_fact_lehrer

32. E. Epel et al. 'Stress may add bite to appetite in women: A laboratory study of stress-induced cortisol and eating behavior', *Psychoneuroendocrinology*, 2001, 26: 37–49. http://www.ncbi.nlm.nih.gov/pmc/articles/PMC3740553/

33. S. Levenstein, *American Journal of Gastroenterology*, May 2000, 95: 1213–1220, http://www.researchgate.net/publication/12507172_Stress_and_exacerbation_in_ulcerative_colitis_a_prospective_study_of_patients_enrolled_in_remission/links/0912f50a6cce1bbb17000000

34. J.F. Cryan, and S.M. O'Mahony, 'The micro-biome gut-brain axis: from bowel to behavior', *Neurogastroenterolgy and motility*, 2011, 23: 187–92 http://spofscc.com/uploads/The_microbiome-gut-brain_axis_from_bowel_to_behavior_1_.pdf

35. F.P. Cappuccio et al., 'Meta-analysis of short sleep duration and obesity in children and adults', *SLEEP*, 2008: 31(5):619–26. http://www.ncbi.nlm.nih.gov/pmc/articles/PMC2398753/

36. N.F. Watson et al., 'Sleep duration and body mass index in twins: a gene-environment interaction', *SLEEP*, 1 May 2012. 35(5):597–603. DOI: 10.5665/sleep.1810. http://www.ncbi.nlm.nih.gov/pubmed/22547885

37. E. McFadden et al., 'The relationship between obesity and exposure to light at night: Cross-sectional analyses of over 100,000 women in the Breakthrough Generations Study', *American Journal of Epidemiology*, 1 August 2014, 180(3):245–50. DOI: 10.1093/age/kuu117.Epub 29 May 2014. http://www.ncbi.nlm.nih.gov/pubmed/24875371?dopt=Abstract

38. M.D.Ying Bao et al., 'Association of nut consumption with total and cause-Specific mortality', *New England Journal of Medicine*, 1 November 2013, 369: 2001–11 DOI: 10.1056/NEJMoa1307352

http://www.nejm.org/doi/full/10.1056/NEJMoa1307352

39. Eric L. Ding et al., 'Chocolate and prevention of cardiovascular disease: A systematic review (London)', 2006, 3: 2.http://www.ncbi.nlm.nih.gov/pmc/articles/PMC1360667/

40. Adam Brickman et al., 'Enhancing dentate gyrus function with dietary flavanols improves cognition in older adults', *Nature Neuroscience*, 2014. DOI:10.1038/nn.3850,26 October 2014. http://www.nature.com/neuro/journal/vaop/ncurrent/full/nn.3850.html

41. S.I. Parvez, K.A. Malik, S. Kang, H.Y. Kim, 'Probiotics and their fermented food products are beneficial for health', *Journal of Applied Microbiology*, June 2006, 100(6):1171–85.http://www.ncbi.nlm.nih.gov/pubmed/16696665

42. Suez, et al., 'Artificial sweeteners induce glucose intolerance by altering the gut microbiota,' *Nature*, 9 October 2014, 514: 181-6. DOI:10.1038/nature13793 http://www.nature.com/nature/journal/v514/n7521/full/nature13793.html#close

43. http://timesofindia.indiatimes.com/home/science/Weight-loss-surgeries-are-not-a-cure-for-diabetes-some-ethics-experts-say/articleshow/44283220.cms

44. Benatti, et al., 'Liposuction induces a compensatory increase of visceral fat which is effectively counteracted by physical activity:A randomized trial', *Journal of Clinical Endocrinology and Metabolism*, July 2012, 97(7):2388–95. DOI: 10.1210/jc.2012-1012. Epub 26 April 2012.

45. R.A. Anderson, 'Chromium and polyphenols from cinnamon improve insulin sensitivity', *Proceedings of the Nutrition Society*, February 2008, 67(1):48–53. http://www.ncbi.nlm.nih.gov/pubmed/18234131

46. Mark Mattson, 'Hormesis defined', *Ageing Research Reviews*, January 2008, 7(1): 1–7., http://www.ncbi.nlm.nih.gov/pmc/articles/PMC2248601/

47. http://www.hiroshimasyndrome.com/radiation-the-no-safe-level-myth.html

48. Catharine Paddock, 'High rates of unnecessary antibiotics prescriptions in US', *Medical News Today*, MediLexicon, Intl., 4 October 2013. Web. 23 October 2014. http://www.medicalnewstoday.com/articles/266998.php

49. Emmanuelle Le Chatelier et al., 'Richness of human gut microbiome correlates with metabolic markers', *Nature* 500, 541–6, 29 August 2013. DOI:10.1038/nature12506http://www.nature.com/nature/journal/v500/n7464/full/nature12506.html

50. http://mobile.nytimes.com/blogs/well/2014/12/01/prescribing-vegetables-not-pills/

51. M.J. Hill, Intestinal flora and endogenous vitamin synthesis', *European Journal of Cancer Prevention*, 6 March 1997, Supplement 1: S43–5.

52. E.I. Giovannucci, Y. Liu, B.W. Hollis, E.B. Rimm. *Archives of Internal Medicine,* 9 June 2008, 168(11): 1174–80. DOI: 10.1001/archinte.168.11.1174., 25-hydroxyvitamin D and risk of myocardial infarction in men: a prospective study. http://www.ncbi.nlm.nih.gov/pubmed/18541825

53. http://www.ncbi.nlm.nih.gov/pubmed/15761167

54. Source: Website www.microbes.orghttp://microbes.org/microscopic-worlds/microbial-habitats

55. James B. Nardi, 'Life in the soil: A guide for naturalists and gardeners', Universites.indiatimes.com/2014-10-15/news/55059624_1_certain-american-farm-products-poultry-imports-wto